HARBORED IN SILENCE

ASPEN PACK
BOOK FOUR

CARRIE ANN RYAN

Harbored in Silence
An Aspen Pack Novel
By: Carrie Ann Ryan

ISBN: 978-1-63695-402-8

Cover Art by Sweet N Spicy Designs

PRAISE FOR CARRIE ANN RYAN....

"Count on Carrie Ann Ryan for emotional, sexy, character driven stories that capture your heart!" – Carly Phillips, NY Times bestselling author

"Carrie Ann Ryan's romances are my newest addiction! The emotion in her books captures me from the very beginning. The hope and healing hold me close until the end. These love stories will simply sweep you away." ~ NYT Bestselling Author Deveny Perry

"Carrie Ann Ryan writes the perfect balance of sweet and heat ensuring every story feeds the soul." - Audrey Carlan, #1 New York Times Bestselling Author

"Carrie Ann Ryan never fails to draw readers in with passion, raw sensuality, and characters that pop off the page. Any book by Carrie Ann is an absolute treat." – New York Times Bestselling Author J. Kenner

"Carrie Ann Ryan knows how to pull your heartstrings and make your pulse pound! Her wonderful Redwood Pack series will draw you in and keep you reading long into the night. I can't wait to see what comes next with the new generation, the Talons. Keep them coming, Carrie Ann!" –Lara Adrian, New York Times bestselling author of CRAVE THE NIGHT

"With snarky humor, sizzling love scenes, and brilliant, imaginative worldbuilding, The Dante's Circle series reads as if Carrie Ann Ryan peeked at my personal wish list!" – NYT Bestselling Author, Larissa Ione

"Carrie Ann Ryan writes sexy shifters in a world full of passionate happily-ever-afters." – *New York Times* Bestselling Author Vivian Arend

"Carrie Ann's books are sexy with characters you can't help but love from page one. They are heat and heart blended to perfection." *New York Times* Bestselling Author Jayne Rylon

Carrie Ann Ryan's books are wickedly funny and deliciously hot, with plenty of twists to keep you guessing. They'll keep you up all night!" USA Today Bestselling Author Cari Quinn

"Once again, Carrie Ann Ryan knocks the Dante's Circle series out of the park. The queen of hot, sexy, enthralling paranormal romance, Carrie Ann is an author not to miss!" *New York Times* bestselling Author Marie Harte

DEDICATION

For those who asked.
Dara righted the wrong.

HARBORED IN SILENCE

A witch on the run who could save the world—or destroy it with one touch

I am who they fear.

The Harvester Death Witch.

The one who holds the power of their fate in my hands.

Or at least...that's what they whisper.

The coven has fallen. The vampires are circling our den. And if we don't find new allies, our Pack won't be able to fight much longer.

On my Alpha's orders, I must find others who hide beneath the shadows for not only our protection, but theirs as well.

Only I'm not alone on my mission.

I brought Cruz back from death once before, and though I know the goddess forbids it, I'd do it again.

Because he's my mate.

And my ending.

CHAPTER ONE

Dara

Black smoke billowed in my face, the explosion ringing through my ears as I tried to suck in a breath, only to cough as inky tendrils of possibly poisoned gas wove its way through my nostrils and down my throat.

I fanned the air in front of my face, choking, as I grasped the edge of my workbench, trying to turn on the exhaust fans. Witchcraft and technology didn't always go hand in hand, but an overhead exhaust fan for your witches' brews really was the only way to go.

Especially since I wasn't an air witch that could do that on my own—I worked in something a little darker.

I shuddered, turning for my water bottle as I wiped

the soot from my eyes. I knew I would need to shower again before I headed out.

This had been my last-ditch effort, one try until I went to my hands and knees once again and begged. Because I *would* beg. At least try—getting anything really hadn't work out for me.

I pressed the button on the top of my water bottle and chugged it back, grateful for the coolness down my throat. I coughed and sputtered as I choked again and spit into the sink, annoyed with myself.

Well, that looks like tar.

What exactly had I just inhaled?

I washed my face in the sink, drank more water, grateful when the smoke began to dissipate. I looked at my cauldron.

It was more of a pot really, one that anyone could make soup in, but I called it my cauldron. That's what a witch did.

At least some witches.

My friends from the other Packs who held power were earth witches and fire witches. Water witches and air witches. I even knew a spirit witch, one who could commune with the dead, and bring forth magic from a knowing and hidden place.

But I was not that.

No, I was a harvester. A death witch.

One who saw and spoke to death and, if the legends

were true, could twist fate and scream into the winds of that goddess-less place.

I was their reckoning, their ending, their doom.

But currently I was covered in soot, had burned part of my hair, and my entire place smelled like rotten eggs.

Good job, Dara, you are the one they all fear. The witch of endless witches.

I rolled my eyes at myself as I cleaned up, knowing that desperation meant I didn't have time to feel sorry for myself.

My people were dying, my Pack wasn't safe.

And if I didn't find a way to stop vampire magic from seeping into our wards, from hiding from us and from killing us in droves, it didn't matter that I might end up killing myself.

All the strength that I held within my bones wouldn't matter, the magic etched within the calcium deposits that had once been lively and full of hope, none of it would matter. Because I would die right alongside my people, and no one would even whisper my name in the end.

I pushed away those thoughts, including the memory of who had been at my house the night before, who had raged at me and spoken truths better left unsaid.

I wouldn't think of him.

I hadn't spoken to him, hadn't answered the questions that needed to be answered.

I had done nothing. Instead, I had broken down when he left, and I knew this was the ending.

Cruz was right.

And I hated that I had to admit that.

There was a knock on the door and I stiffened, worried once again.

It wouldn't be Cruz. He wouldn't be returning. Not after he left, derision and confusion within his eyes.

He knew. He knew the answers to his own questions, but they weren't ones that we wanted to speak of, weren't ones that would make everything better and would save the Packs and make warmth and rainbows shoot out of his ass.

No, none of that would happen.

I was going to pretend. Because it was what I was good at.

The doorbell rang and I winced, the sound echoing within my ears. I hadn't even realized I had a headache, probably because I always had one these days.

The magic of the wards was draining me, and I was exhausted.

Everybody knew it, but they didn't say it. They just gave me pitying and hopeful looks. Because they were putting themselves into the wards too. The wards just happened to be fighting me a little bit more.

I opened the door to two of my best friends. The two people who were going to help me, at least that's what they said. And I wanted to believe that they could. That they would.

But I didn't know if they were going to be enough.

"You look horrible," Wynter said as she shook her head. She reached forward and gripped my hand before leaning to kiss my cheek. "And you taste like soot." She scrunched her cute little nose and wiped her lips.

I loved Wynter. She was a human living within the Pack, for her own reasons, and while she had a day job, and even had a place outside the den, she also had one within the wards. She fought with us, was part of us, and had a connection to the Pack just like I did.

We weren't wolves or one of the other types of shifters, but we were Pack nonetheless. She had bright blue eyes that held knowledge that I didn't quite understand. She was human, and yet I felt like her soul was far older than anyone else's on this earth.

Or maybe that was just my headache speaking. Her honey-brown hair billowed around her face, and she looked gorgeous and fragile.

She could be hurt far easier than all of us, and only had a weapon in her hand to protect herself. No claws, no strength beyond her human mortality, and no magic.

Beside her stood a lynx and one of my other best friends.

Wren scowled at me and held out her hand. "Okay, give me your hand."

"You know it doesn't work well with me. I just end up taking your energy."

"And you think I care? We have bonds. And you're

going to let me help. And then you're going to shower because dear goddess, you need it."

I snorted, a smile playing on my face, and it was exactly what the Healer of the Aspen Pack wanted. She latched onto my distraction, pouring her healing warmth into me.

Magic sizzled up my skin and I sighed, taking in the life that she sent.

I was death, the Healer was life, two opposing forces that shouldn't be friends, but all of it was a circle. There was no ending or beginning when it came to life and death, they were one in the eyes of the goddess.

Wren smiled, squeezed my hand, and I sighed with a warmth that I rarely felt.

"Thank you. That helped the headache."

"Not anything else, but we both know I'm trying."

I shook my head and pulled them both into the house. "You should stop trying. It just weakens you, and we need all of your strength. Especially if I can't get these wards fixed."

We had patched the wards that protected the den from outside forces repeatedly. They had fallen in battle more than once, leaving the innocent unprotected and frightened. It didn't matter that every time we found a new way to protect ourselves, vampires, humans, or other rival Packs took them down.

We changed the way things had been made, put new

magics into them, but with a certain magical group holding back, they'd weakened once again.

Hence why my friends were there, and why the trepidation that lay within me wouldn't stop.

"Go shower, and then we'll go with you."

"I can go alone. You don't need to go and witness this." I rolled my eyes as I stripped off my shirt right in front of them, and continued to strip on my way to the bathroom.

I wasn't a shifter, didn't need to get naked in order to shift into a different being. Shifters within the Aspen Pack were all fine with nudity. It was just something that was a part of them, and when you walked within the forest along the trails of shifters, you saw naked men and women often. You saw naked shifters often. You became immune to the nudity.

I was used to it, and these were my friends, we had danced naked under the moon when I called magic. Wynter might be human, but she had joined in, and we had laughed. As a shifter herself, Wren was even more blasé about nudity than me.

Wynter sighed and picked up my clothes behind me. I shook my head and jumped into the shower.

I was quick about it, knowing we didn't have much time if we wanted to get this over with.

"I can clean up after myself."

"You just left a trail of clothes, so no, you can't. I'll start laundry." Wynter mumbled around my house, picking up the messes I had made.

I was normally a much tidier person, but recently I'd been devoting all of my strength toward finding magical ways to counteract the vampires' poisons.

My workspace, save for the new sooted area that would be cleaned up soon, was pristine. I knew where every part of my spells were, every ounce of every ingredient, but the rest of my house needed a good scrubbing.

"I'm going to start on your dishes. Though you don't have much here..." Wren began. "Which worries me because I don't think you've been eating enough."

"I'm eating," I said, rinsing out the conditioner from my hair. It was a quick job, and I knew that I was losing more hair than normal. But every ounce of my magic was being put into the wards, to protect our people, and it still wasn't enough.

It was never enough.

When the vampires had first shown themselves, everything changed. For my entire life, and for the centuries that shifters had been secret, we hadn't realized vampires were real.

But a few decades ago, when a nearby Pack took down the demon threatening us all, things changed. Another demon, at least as far as we could tell, had created vampires in his own image. I still wasn't sure how it had happened, or their overall goal, but they were trying to kill us. Trying to take out those magic users and shifters that didn't agree with them, so they could rule the supernaturals. They wanted to pit humans against us so we were fighting amongst ourselves before the vampires took over everything. Or perhaps it was the demon who wanted to rule.

I knew that vampires were made from humans who either wanted power or were forced into it. It took training, and the control of the higher-powered vampires in order to bring the mindless vampire hordes into submission. Once a vampire learned to control his power, his thirst for blood and agony, he could rule other vampires.

They were just as strong as a shifter, sometimes stronger if they had their own vampire magic in their arsenal. They used to be able to damage our wards, and we had stopped them, and they pivoted to find another way.

I was truly afraid that they had found a witch. That was what was always unsaid. That the witches had turned to the vampires' side.

Because the coven was no longer working with the shifters.

Years ago, before I was even born, the witches had come together as a coven locally, and they ruled the entire Pacific Northwest.

They came together and decided who was allowed to be a witch, who was allowed to have their power, and who had to be hidden.

It was no surprise that as a non-elemental witch, I wasn't allowed to be part of the inner circle. And over time they had pushed out anyone connected to Packs through mating or family. They only wanted those of pure blood, only those with power that they thought they understood. But even while they had done that, they had always worked with the Packs to ensure that the wards of every magical creature were safe. They were safe from the prying eyes of the human governments that wanted to control us, safe from humans who wanted to hurt us. Safe from other Packs. And witches were safe from those who were stronger than them, or who wanted their magic for their own gain.

All of that with the council had occurred before I was born, and they had fought to protect all of us.

But now the coven no longer worked with the council, and those magic users either had to hide who they were, or work in factions that didn't have the power to organize or control.

We were dying, and I needed to stop it.

"Are you ready to go?" I asked as I ran my hands through my wet hair. I muttered a spell under my breath, using the small power of air that I held. It wasn't truly air magic, but it was the opposite of life. Death and life were one, so I was able to use the power of world and energy to do small things. My hair dried instantly, and Wynter just rolled her eyes.

"Seriously, you look amazing. I hate you."

Wren scowled at me, and I knew she saw the fact that I couldn't hide the dark circles underneath my eyes, even with a glamour, and my cheekbones were a little more pronounced than usual.

I knew Wynter saw it too, but we didn't mention it. Not when there was nothing to stop it.

It didn't help that it wasn't only the wards that were draining the life from me.

There was something else.

Someone else.

I shook that thought away as the girls moved forward.

"Let's go, especially before we get told we're not allowed to," Wren said with a sigh.

We were going to see the coven. One last-ditch effort. But because the coven no longer wanted to work with the Pack, and were adamant about it, my Alpha could warn us away from it. So as long as he didn't know where we were going, as long as those in the Pack hierarchy didn't know, we could still do this. We could try to protect our people.

I would beg for help if I had to.

We got in the car and were waved through past the sentries.

"Chase is going to know where we're going. He always does," Wren said with a sigh.

"True, but he hasn't told us not to go, so I'm going to take that as permission," Wynter added.

"I'm sure Cruz and Steele know as well. And they'll yell at us."

Chase was our Alpha, Cruz the Heir—second in command, one who helped hold the mantle of Pack bonds. Steele was our Enforcer, in charge of the outside security of the Pack. Any outside forces that came at us would alert his Pack bonds. The fact that we had been in constant battles and wars since the vampires came out had to be stressing his own powers. I didn't know how he dealt with it, but he did. Because he was the Enforcer, and that was what he did.

We made our way out of the forest and into the city, where the coven was located. They used to be within the forest with us, hiding from the humans. But when magic had begun to come out into the public, when the shifters had, they'd had to hide in different ways.

"I still can't believe that they live in a townhouse here," Wynter said with a sigh.

My lips twisted in a sneer. "Because the new coven didn't want to be hidden."

"Do you still believe that the new coven hierarchy killed the others?" Wren asked softly, her Healer heart breaking.

"Yes. Those who created this coven originally wouldn't have left us like this. They wouldn't have disappeared into the night without a word." Hope twisted inside me, and I swallowed hard, the grief of my friends' deaths still wrapped around me. "They could have run, could have been forced into it by having their families threatened. But nobody has sent word. Nobody has heard from them. I fully believe that the new coven leaders killed the old ones. Because they wanted power."

"And now we're going there to beg for help. For them

not to renege on their prior promises," Wynter said with a sigh. "Sounds like fun."

"It sounds like we should have brought more firepower," Wren said with a wince.

"And if we did that, they would've taken it as an act of war. If I go as a witch with my two friends to beg, maybe it'll be enough."

"I don't like the thought of you having to beg. They should just want to do this."

"They should, but they don't. They pushed out everybody with a connection to the past. Everybody who wasn't as *special* as they are."

We were silent after that because there was nothing else to say. We had gone over this countless times, and I wasn't sure what else there was to do.

When we pulled into the small neighborhood and saw the house at the end of the drive, hidden amongst trees, something strummed along my magic, and I knew something was wrong.

I opened the door, not bothering to turn off the car, and ran toward the wrongness, my soul aching as death once again sung toward me, calling me.

Wren cursed under her breath, following me, running even faster. She wasn't the strongest wolf, but the power of Healer ebbed within her. She was a shifter and naturally faster and stronger than me. "I smell blood."

Wynter was right behind us, running quickly, just not

as fast as Wren could. She had her blades in her hands, in open view of anyone who was watching, but it didn't matter. I held out my hands, my power strumming along my palms.

It was a dark orb, power of death. I didn't kill with it, not unless I had to, but I could stun, I could push back. My power was unlike anyone else's, but I used it how I could.

"Something's wrong. Wynter, call the others. Get the Pack here."

"I'm not letting you go alone. There could be vampires in there."

I turned to her for a moment before looking at Wren. "Do you scent them? Feel them? Because I don't."

The Healer looked torn before she shook her head. "No. I only scent blood...and magic. But no vampires." A pause. "Dara."

"We don't have a choice," I murmured.

Wynter cursed and pulled out her phone, Wren between us, then I moved.

The door was ajar, the magical wards that protected the coven from the outside world broken. But they hadn't just been broken. No, they were tattered and jagged shards of magic that pierced my skin as I moved forward, unable to keep me out.

I tasted death on the air, not just blood, not just magic, but *death.*

I had brought someone back before, something the

goddess had forbidden me to do, but I had done it. I wouldn't do it again to others, I wouldn't do it here.

I walked past the blood and the death of the coven who had forsaken us, and knew that whoever had killed them wasn't our friend.

This was not the enemy of my enemy, no, this was death itself.

A rasping sound hit my ear while Wren and Wynter went to each fallen witch, trying to help. But I knew they were dead, I could feel their death.

I moved towards the rasping breath where Henrick lay like a broken doll over a torn armchair.

The coven leader—the one who hated us the most—looked at me, his eyes wide, blood seeping from the corner of his mouth, and I felt only pity.

Nobody deserved to die like this.

He held his hand over his stomach, trying to keep what was inside *inside*. Everything stank of death, of what was to come. But I didn't say anything. And so he moved my hand over his heart, and pushed in magic. His eyes widened, and that was when he knew.

I was the death witch, but I was not death. I couldn't control it.

"It was her," he whispered.

I leaned forward, doing my best to save him. I hated him, hated what he had done and what he stood for. But I would not let him die in agony. I knew death called to him, and there was nothing I could do, not without sacrificing my own soul—and his. And that was the crux. I would control his soul if I wasn't careful, and he was too close to death for me not to. But I could ease his pain. As I did so, he reached out with his free hand, his bloody fingerprints on my skin.

"It was her. She promised to help us. And she killed us." Blood burbled from his mouth as I tried to understand what was going on.

"Who was it? Who did this?" I asked, holding his hand as tightly as I could. There was nothing more I could do. He could feel no more pain, but I couldn't stave off death, not without risking his soul.

"It was her. The coven is dead. And it was her."

And with that, the coven leader died, right along with the coven. Death kissed my cheek and left me kneeling in a pool of blood, with the promise of what was to come.

The coven was dead. The humans and their laws would be here soon. The Pack would be close by.

And death beckoned.

CHAPTER TWO

Cruz

SHE DID WHAT?

That was the phrase that constantly ran through my mind in a loop.

Dara had run into a house that scented of dark magic and blood.

Check.

Dara had done some form of magic on her own, the likes which nobody could explain to me, and hadn't said a thing.

Check.

Dara had been kneeling in the blood of our enemy,

head bent over the coven leader, when I'd run into the townhouse.

Check.

The entire coven was dead, and it stank of vampires and dark magic. And Dara was in the middle of it.

Check.

Dara had come to this place on her own without letting anybody know and bringing two other Packmates with her. Two other Packmates who were not fighters.

Check.

I was going to kill the woman who might be my mate.

That was it. She might be a death witch, but I was going to be her death.

I could not believe I had walked in and shouted at the woman who could be my mate standing in blood.

And I didn't shout.

I was the calm and collected one when everyone else felt like death was coming. That was what I did.

But when I'd seen her, I'd lost my damn mind.

"What the hell are you doing?" I said, and she rolled on me.

"Trying to do what I could. You're here, so help me clean up this mess. We don't need the humans to find it."

And then she passed out. I cursed, catching her before she landed in the gore.

She had used too much magic, like always. Because she only took care of others and never thought about herself.

What was I supposed to do with a mate like that?

Nothing, that's what. There was nothing for me to do with a mate who not only didn't want me but was trying to kill herself in the process.

My wolf paced, shuddering. Because it knew the truth.

Because even if she continued this, if she stopped this and found a way to protect the Pack without killing herself along the way, I knew I would be that last step.

And neither one of us wanted to think about that.

Wren was there in an instant, her lynx pulling at my wolf, needing my power as Heir. That was what I was good for, the legacy for our Alpha, Chase, and to help push power into those who needed it.

Wren wasn't exactly a submissive, but she wasn't a dominant either. All of her power came from her inner strength and the fact that she was a Healer. So she used what she could to push healing into Dara, but when she cursed under her breath for the fifth time in just a few minutes, I knew it didn't work the way that it should. I could sense that Dara was just sleeping at that point, exhausted, but whatever magic that Dara held didn't always mesh well with Pack magic.

Another strike against whatever the goddess had foretold for us.

The thing with mating was that you had potentials. Yes, we were fated mates. Yes, the goddess had put us together so we could see who we could be together. Our souls would combine, and we would find passion and hope and prosperity. And all that other bullshit that came with fated mates.

But it was never forced. It was a potential. I could find another potential in my long lifetime. I had friends who had found two mates in their lifetimes, and had ended up being able to choose the one that was perfect for them because of circumstances that wouldn't make sense to anyone outside of our world.

I had to keep telling myself that Dara wasn't mine.

When they took her away and left me behind, along with Steele and a few others to clean up the mess in the estate, I wondered why the hell the goddess hated me so much.

I had yelled at Dara, and that was the last thing I said before she passed out and left me here surrounded by death and wondered how long it would take to remove blood from carpet.

"I miss the old coven," Steele grumbled. "It was easier when we had the witches to clean stuff like this up. Right now, I don't think Dara could lift her pinky, let alone the blood from this carpet."

I scowled over at my best friend and Enforcer. "Don't you dare ask Dara to help with this. She already did some whammy on Henrick, trying to save him or some bullshit. And now she's hurt and unconscious. She doesn't think about herself at all."

Steele raised a single brow which spoke volumes.

"If you're done with that, why don't you take a breath? Because what the hell, man?"

"What about the other witches from the Talon Pack? The Redwoods? They should have people."

"We're on it. Don't worry. We will clean this up. Although I'm surprised that humans aren't here already, thanks to the smell." Steele scrunched his nose, and my wolf hummed in agreement.

It stank of death and all of the disgusting things that came with it. It wasn't just blood. And these people had died horribly.

I might not have liked any of them, but I didn't want them dead.

Nobody deserved to die like this.

They had become their own ending, and it didn't make any sense.

"There was a geas." I looked up as Cassius came through, soldier and dominant wolf and friend.

Cassius nodded at us and frowned at the tablet in his hand. "Novah mentioned it to me, as one of the council members had it in their notes. Just like we use wards, and our old wards used to be able to have a 'don't look here' or something like to prevent humans from finding us, the witches had one too."

My eyes widened. "In the middle of a city? That's got some balls on it."

Cassius snorted. "Pretty much. But they haven't figured it out yet."

"So the authorities won't be here. Meaning we have time to figure out exactly what the witches were up to." That left a metallic taste in my mouth, annoyed with myself for even thinking it.

"These witches," Steele chided gently. "These witches who decided to go against the former coven."

"Did we ever find out what happened to Diana or Amelia?" I asked, my voice quiet, not sure I wanted to know the answer.

Cassius shook his head. "No. Either the witches hid their bodies, or they hid themselves well enough from whatever other crap these people were up to that we couldn't find them."

"I wouldn't blame them for leaving and hiding. I just hope they get back to us at some point. Although if Henrick's last words were true, that means whoever they were working with turned on them." I clenched my jaw, as Cassius nodded tightly. "Turned on them and took everything from them. The coven is gone. No more."

I couldn't help but think of Dara, about the fact that she had been here most likely to ask for help, help from a coven that had shunned her and had never let her be part of them. She was a witch, goddess damn it. And yet they hadn't let her be part of them.

"It was going to be hard enough to continue this war without the coven, but that was just when we were fighting with them. Now that they're gone completely? I don't know what we're going to do."

"That will be a question for Chase and the other Alphas. Let's clean up here, be careful of any traps that the coven's enemy or the coven themselves may have laid for us, and then we'll get back to the den. I don't like being gone for too long."

They nodded and we moved around, cleaning up the death, which lay heavy in the air and I knew would never fade away.

*

By the time we made it back to the den, dawn was on its way to the Pacific Northwest. I rubbed my temples and knew that sleep wouldn't be coming anytime soon. Not when we had a Pack council meeting coming up.

Not everyone there would be part of the hierarchy, but since I was the Heir, I had to be there. I had to tell them what I saw, and we needed to make plans for what to do about this.

But first, I needed to shower.

I resisted the urge to stop by Dara's place though, to ensure that she was actually resting.

It should not be my problem if she was sleeping or not. When I went to her and asked her why we hadn't spoken of being mates, she had rebuffed me, pushed me away.

I wasn't going to force her into taking me. Into

believing in what we could have, because I didn't even know what that could be in the first place.

The goddess had made a mistake.

I couldn't be with a woman who didn't want me.

And I wasn't going to be forced into a situation where I needed to be bonded again.

I was already part of the Aspen Pack for those reasons. I wasn't going to force a mating where it clearly wasn't wanted. Nor was I going to let what had happened stand between us forever, though.

There were answers that needed to come out. And not just about our mating.

I jumped into the shower, grateful to wash off the scent of blood and death, as I rubbed my hand over my chest.

I remembered dying.

It was odd to think that I could remember death. No, that wasn't quite true. I didn't remember death. I only remembered dying, gasping that last breath as vampire black-splintered magic slid into my chest and took me away from this earth.

I remembered that pain, the agony. And then I remembered a gasping breath, fiery burning wrath wrapping around me, and looking up into Dara's coal-black eyes as she screamed for me.

Only her mouth had been open, but no sound came out.

We had been on the battlefield, and I'd felt my bond to my Alpha, to my Pack, break.

I didn't know what to say about that.

Dara had saved my life, had brought me back from death. Not the brink of it, but actual death, and now my mate was dying.

There was something between us, not a mating bond. No, neither one of us would allow that. But there was something, and as I continued in this existence I was afraid I knew the answer.

Dara was dying because of me.

All because she had saved my life. And I didn't know how to fix that, or if there was even a way to fix that.

I shook my head, telling myself once again that there was no point in rehashing this. When we finally did, we would probably end up blowing apart half of the damn den, but we'd figure it out.

First, though, we needed magic.

For the wards, the den, and to fight against these vampire powers.

And I wasn't going to lie. A small part of me also wanted that magic to help Dara. No, that was indeed a lie. It wasn't just a small part.

We needed witches, Dara needed witches. So, despite the fact that we were never going to be truly mates, I would do all that I could to make sure she got them.

My phone buzzed and I looked down, noting that I was

being summoned to the Pack meeting. It wouldn't be all of us, as not even the entire Pack lived within the den wards, but it would be enough of us with the power to make choices for each other, and it was important that I be there.

I rolled my shoulders back, working the exhaustion out of my muscles, but it didn't matter that I hadn't slept the night before. We needed to get through this.

I grabbed some coffee and made my way to Chase and Skye's home.

They had moved into this place after they mated. Chase had always wanted to live in a smaller home, despite the fact that he had to have these meetings at his place. Our Beta, Audrey, had been hosting some of the meetings at her place in the interim, but now as a mated couple, the Alpha pair had more space for all of us.

It was early enough that people were either still asleep or just getting ready for their day and weren't out and about. The word hadn't spread yet about the coven's demise, and I was grateful. I didn't want to deal with that. I had a feeling that would fall to Audrey. As Beta, it was her job to ensure the safety and needs of the den structure. I was there to support her as Heir. Hell, my entire role was to support. My Pack bonds were similar to Chase. I helped him deal with the day-to-day business of having to note every single instant of hope, happiness, anger, and fear of the Pack, and the responsibility that came with being Alpha.

I aided our Healer like I had earlier, and if he ever let

me, I would do the same for our Omega. Hayes, the big polar bear shifter who grunted more often than not, refused to let any of us help him. It didn't matter that sometimes during the days of war and darkness we all felt like we were fading, and Hayes was the only one propping us up. No, he wouldn't let us help so we were forced to stand by and watch. But just like all of us, we had to deal with our own bullshit. And he was really good at it.

"Oh good, you're here. I was afraid that you would still be at that place." I turned to see Wynter coming towards me. I held out my arm, and she sank into my side, hugging me tightly. I still didn't know why this human was part of our den, as far as I could tell she had no ties to any of the shifters, but she had always been here. Part of us. And my wolf liked it. It liked protecting her. We were friends, nothing more, and I was glad for it. But I still scowled down at her, tapping her nose with my finger. "What the hell were you thinking?"

She scowled at me, that fiery temper of hers adorable. She would probably burn me alive for even saying that out loud so I would keep those thoughts to myself. She was getting good at blades though.

"I was thinking that Dara was going to do whatever she could to save us. And I wasn't going to let my friend go alone. Neither was Wren. So we went. We had a shifter, a witch, and little old human me. But I have knives, and I know how to use them."

I kissed the top of her head as we made our way

toward Chase's house. "You are good with knives. Adalyn helping?"

Adalyn was a Central wolf now, part of the mated triad of the Alpha hierarchy. It was so weird to think that she wasn't a Packmate anymore, even though the four Packs in our area were part of an alliance. As such, the Pack bonds were starting to blend in a way that I had never heard of before.

In essence, the Redwoods and the Talons were practically one Pack with two Alphas. Now the Centrals and Aspens were blending as well. My wolf didn't know what to think about it, but it liked the idea of more protection, and more to protect. The human part of me knew it was going to be a pain in the ass if these Alphas ever got annoyed with each other. But so far they seemed to be getting along, and I got along with the other Heirs. So we figured it out. One war at a time.

I led Wynter inside and nodded at Cassius where he sat in the corner, looking as exhausted as I felt. His mate Novah handed a cup of coffee to him and smiled at me.

Hayes was in the kitchen, along with Wren and Steele. They talked in low tones with each other, and I nodded at them before going to sit next to Skye. The former Redwood member, now my Alpha female, smiled at me and rested her head on my shoulder.

"I'm tired. But we're fine."

"I guess we're as fine as we're going to be," I grumbled.

Audrey and Gavin walked in just then, nodding at us, with trays of muffins in hand.

"This is the best we could do. The maternals weren't happy that we stole so many muffins, but I have a feeling that they knew we were going to meet." Gavin shrugged as he spoke, then handed over the trays. "I don't think they know exactly what happened, but considering you guys were out late, they know it wasn't good."

I looked around and noticed who was absent, and held back a curse.

And it wasn't just the fact that she could have been my mate. No, it was the fact that she wasn't here. And neither was another who used to be with us.

None of us spoke it, but we knew Lily was gone. She had to be. We hadn't found her body, but there had been no ransom note, no scent. We had searched in the weeks since we last saw our witch Packmate. But she was gone. There were no Pack bonds left. It was as if she had been sliced away from us, though we hadn't had a chance to say goodbye.

"I'm here, I'm here," Dara said as she walked in. My wolf perked up, wanting to see her, to touch her. But I didn't. Instead, I sat straighter, trying to act nonchalant, even as Hayes gave me a look.

Oh, the Omega knew. I was pretty sure he was the only one that did. You couldn't hide your emotions from the damn Omega. But I didn't want anyone else to know.

Not when I knew it was only going to end badly.

Chase settled Dara into her seat, then began to go over things. Skye sighed into my side and let out a breath.

We weren't starting the meeting yet, just reviewing a few other things, so I looked at her.

"What's wrong?" I asked. "Beyond the obvious."

She gave me a sad smile and shook her head.

"Baby?" Chase asked, and they all turned to us. Skye reddened and shook her head.

Skye wasn't a submissive or dominant. She was a Gamma. She was the balance for a broken Alpha and a broken Pack. My wolf wanted to ensure that she kept that balance, even if I was still trying to come to terms with it.

"Today's just a bad day for other things," she whispered, and Chase frowned at her before he cursed under his breath and stood up quickly. I moved out of the way, trading seats with him so I ended up by Dara, doing my best not to pay attention to her, as Chase wrapped his mate up into his arms and murmured to her.

I frowned looking around as Hayes let out a pained sigh, rubbing his hand over his chest.

I could only imagine the emotions in the room.

Skye wiped the tears from her cheeks, waved her mate off, and smiled up at us. "I'm sorry. It's just the anniversary of the battle with the general. When we lost Blake, my cousin."

We all sat in silence, and I remembered her cousin. He was the son of North and Lexi, the cousin of Parker, our Voice of the Wolves. He had been a strong fighter, a guy with a great smile, and I had only met him a few times. Our Pack had been different then, hidden in the shadows, about to go dark and break.

He had died protecting his family and it wasn't fair. And now we were in another war, with another enemy, and it felt as if we didn't have enough time to grieve our fallen, to remember who we had lost along the way.

"Let's talk about other things. Things we can fix. Because we can't do anything else right now."

I nodded at Skye's words, and then I told them what I saw, and Cassius and Steele added in their own parts. Wynter, Wren, and Dara spoke as well, and we laid it all out there.

"The coven is gone," Dara began. I looked at her, my wolf in pain, agony slicing through him. But I ignored him.

"What does this mean?" Audrey asked, holding up her hand to quiet the room since everyone spoke at once. "I know it means that they're gone. I know it means that we're fucked. But what can we do? For the witches. And us, but there are other witches out there, right?"

Dara's eyes darkened, and she nodded tightly. "We need to find them. And I have an idea."

I had a feeling I was not going to like whatever idea my mate had.

CHAPTER THREE

Dara

Everyone turned to me and I swallowed hard, the tension thick in the air and twisting around my spine. Cruz stiffened at my side, and I wanted to turn to him, to explain to him.

There was that small part of me that wanted him to see me. To *know* me. To want to understand me.

But there was the rest of me that knew that he needed to stay away. For his sake, and for mine.

We barely knew each other. I knew he was the Heir to the Pack, the one who protected us. The one who put his all into our Pack even if he didn't realize it. He was the quiet one behind the Alpha, the one others turned to when they didn't want to bother or pressure the Alpha or Beta or anyone else.

I didn't know his family. Didn't know his history. Nobody did. Perhaps his best friends, but not me.

It was odd to think that the fates had decided we should be together, that our souls would be bonded as one and we would find an eternity of bliss and happiness or whatever else the fuck they thought it would be.

Only, I didn't know him. He didn't know me. He didn't know how I had joined the Pack or where I had come from. We'd fought side by side, shared meals, become Packmates, but we didn't *know* each other the way we should. We only knew about our potential, and that was the problem with the goddess and the way that she played with our lives.

I cringed inwardly at that thought.

Cruz leaned into me slightly, pressing his arm to mine. I didn't have a shifter inside me, didn't have the ability to calm myself like that. But I could sense his wolf. That was odd though, that had never happened to me before, but I knew. That this was his wolf, sensing my stress and needing to protect me in some way.

I huffed out a breath and spoke. "We need witches. We need to protect our den and the dens around us."

"We've tried that, and even before this happened to the coven, we didn't have enough," Audrey said, not unkindly.

I nodded, looking at the rest of them. I usually didn't

have a problem speaking in front of others, telling them what I thought. But right then I wanted to hide. And then Cruz pressed into me again and I felt relief.

I wasn't quite sure how I felt about that, but I didn't have time to worry about it. Not when I needed to focus.

"You're right, it didn't work. The witches that we have in the dens are strong. Even those without the magic reserves some of us have, every single person who has helped has been strong. Has pushed and done their best to ensure that our Pack was safe. But we don't have everything that we need. And the coven is a large part of that." I paused, an odd sense of shame sliding over me. "*Was* a large part of that."

There was a moment of silence as we mourned the dead, even though they had been our enemy. Death wasn't something that was right in any case. It didn't matter that I was an actual death witch, could hold death in my hands. I didn't like the idea of loss surrounding me.

"We have earth, fire, air, water, and spirit witches on our sides. And I'm a harvester death witch." Nobody flinched around me, they just nodded.

It was a novel idea, the fact that they weren't afraid of me. At least not so much that I noticed. Which was amazing, because when I first joined the Pack, they had been afraid of me, of what I could do, because they didn't know. The fact that I hadn't known either probably hadn't helped.

"But there are more."

"More harvester witches?" Cruz asked, his voice soft though everyone in the room heard him.

I shook my head. "I'm not sure about that. Witch magic is hereditary, as is evidenced by Nico being an earth witch and a shifter from all of his parents," I said, speaking of part of the Alpha triad in the Central Pack. "But there are other powers we could use. I know I probably shouldn't have, but I spoke to Hannah, and she's working on bringing in all of the elemental witches that she can find, now that we don't have the coven telling us no."

Hannah was the former Healer of the Redwood Pack, and an earth witch, as well as Nico's mother.

I looked towards Chase and cringed. "I'm sorry for not asking you first. But things needed to happen quickly, and well, I didn't have time to ask permission."

Chase's lips twitched and Cruz stiffened at my side, leaning forward so he was slightly in between me and the Alpha. I didn't know what that meant, and I didn't even think he realized he had done it. That was all his wolf, and he probably wasn't going to be happy when he realized it.

"That's good. And as it happens, I've already spoken to the Redwood Alpha, so we know that she's searching for more elementals."

"There are many witches out there, elementals and not, who weren't allowed to be part of the coven because they didn't fit in with the image that the new coven members were imposing. And even before that, with Diana and Amelia and the others, they didn't want to be part of the coven. They didn't want an organization to tell them what to do, or to put a target on their backs. I get that."

I looked around as that familiar sense of loss hit me from speaking those women's names. "I wasn't coven, at first because I didn't want to be, and then because they didn't want my magic. But I have Pack. The Aspens, you let me join you. And it might have put a target on my back, just like others were fearing, but I'd rather be here with that target than not." I took a deep breath and continued to speak before anyone could respond. "And while we're discussing that, there are others like me, like I said. Others who aren't elementals. Other witches that use powers that might not be so traditional as herbs and air and wind and earth. Others that the coven didn't want out in the open because they feared what the humans might say. But they're good people. They just have powers that scare others."

"Are they safe to be around our den?" Steele asked, ever the Enforcer.

"The people that I need to find, the ones who are underground and try to stay out of the way, were my friends in the past, or helped me in some way when I was searching for a home. I wouldn't call all of them my friends because I don't know them as well anymore. But I used to trust them, and I hope I can again. But these aren't the people that you can ask for help over the phone." I stared at my Alpha. "I'd like your permission to go and speak to them. To find these witches that I know can help build a stronger ward. I know it's asking a lot. Hannah and the other elemental witches will be here, to try to stabilize what we have, but I can't watch us fail because we're not using our resources. And I think I can find better resources. So please, let me help."

"You're going to go alone, on this trip finding witches that you haven't spoken to in how long? Witches with powers that we don't even know. No. Not happening."

I turned to Cruz as people stopped talking and stared at him. And then at me, and then between the two of us.

My hackles rose and I narrowed my gaze at him. Nobody knew we were mates, *potential* mates, and nobody needed to know. But if he kept acting like this, the dominant asshole who wanted to protect me even though he had no idea what the fuck he was doing, people were going to figure it out soon.

"You're not my Alpha. You don't get to tell me what to do. So fuck off."

I smiled as I said it, and Steele whistled between his teeth.

Hayes looked at me, raised those big brows of his, and I winced.

Oh no, there was *someone* who knew. The Omega always knew.

"While I love watching the two of you fight, you're both right." We whirled on Chase, who snorted and said, "Don't look at me like that, I'm more dominant than both of you. So lower your gaze, before I have to get all wolfy on you."

Cruz growled, and he did lower his gaze. It was his wolf pushing at him, and I understood it. I had to balance my own power, but Cruz had to do it as well.

"Who are you going to find? What is your plan?" Chase asked.

I nodded. "I know of five witches. I think they can help."

"What do they do? How do you think it can help?" Audrey held up her hands as I turned to her. "I believe you. I will do all that I can to help you. I promise. But I want to know. Because I want you to be safe, too."

I pressed my lips together and nodded, an odd warmth filling me. I wasn't good at being friends. I was trying. I had girlfriends that I was working with and trying not to ruin those relationships, but sometimes my magic got the better of me, just like their wolves and cats did.

"I've known Jade the longest, so I want to find her as quickly as possible. I have feelers out, I've always had those out by the way, to know where they are. Jade is a fire witch, but a little different than the fire witches we know." I shook my head. "I can't tell you all of their powers other than the fact that as long as I've known them they have done their best to use them for good. Or at least on the twisted side of good."

They all stared at me, and I shrugged. "You use your claws and your fangs to rip into flesh and to fight vampires.

You all have your animals deep inside you, fighting yourselves. We're not human, none of us. I have a power within me that calls to death. And I might be a harvester, but I don't harvest your deaths." And I wouldn't, despite the fact that I could. But they didn't need to know that. "We all have the twisted sides of us that we fight against, or lean into. But I believe that if we find them, it'll be worth the risk."

My body started shaking, and once again something came over me that I'd tried to hold back.

My head tilted back, and I knew that my eyes were glowing but unfocused.

Wren moved to me quickly, though I knew the others were near. "It's the goddess. It's happened before."

My magic pushed at me, and I fisted my hands at my side, trying not to throw up.

"Death is righting a wrong for a past forsaken. The lost son will return, and the tears of pain and agony will dry. Though the sacrifice of cost of an action will never be equal, but will return threefold."

I shuddered as a voice that wasn't my own escaped from my mouth, and I fell back into Cruz. Wren held my hand, pushing healing energy into me as Cruz held me tightly, his hands going up and down my arms, his chin over my head as I shook, my tongue tasting metal.

"What was that? What the hell was that?" Steele asked.

I pulled back from Wren, but didn't move from Cruz.

I couldn't right then, and honestly I didn't want to. Yes, it was wrong, and I was probably going to regret it later, but I needed his touch. It calmed me, soothed me. It was a drug that I couldn't stop, couldn't push away from. And he didn't pull away either.

Hopefully the others would just see it as one Pack-mate comforting another, and not us fighting what we had tried to push away for so long.

I ached, but this couldn't be more. It would never be more.

"Sometimes your goddess has a funny idea of what it means to be close to death. Sometimes she likes to speak through me. It's happened once before, at least in front of Wren. Sorry. But apparently we're going to right some wrongs. Not that I know what that means."

"You're not going out alone, even if you wanted to. Not if you're going to be spewing the moon goddess out of nowhere," Cruz grumbled. I pulled away from him, only now realizing I'd been sitting on his lap.

"Again, don't tell me what to do. I'm fine. She doesn't do that often. That was just weird." I rubbed my temple as the others began to plan. I tried to tune them out, my headache coming harder.

"We need to keep our den safe," Chase began, and I looked at him. "We need magic—our wolves have it, as do the other shifters and witches in this Pack. The coven is gone, and I don't know if you want to rebuild it, that's not something I can decide, but the witches and those magic users are the ones that can." He paused and looked directly at me. "And those with power who have been hiding for fear of persecution from the coven? They need protection too."

My heart filled as Skye looked up at her mate and kissed his cheek.

"You're a good Alpha," she whispered, and I grinned, despite the pressure of the situation.

"You are," I agreed.

"She's not going alone," Cruz said. "If she wants to do this, she's not going alone."

I bristled but Chase looked between us and nodded. "Good. I wasn't planning on it. You're going with her."

I froze. "What?"

"I have things to do here, there are other soldiers that can go with her."

I ignored the pain at those words, the fact that he could just brush me off like that even though he wanted to tell me what to do.

"I'm sure you feel you could do all of this. But we can handle it here. Keep Dara safe." He turned to me as I opened my mouth. "Keep Cruz safe. Find those that can help us, and help them as well. If the goddess is speaking to you right now, which by the way is something we're going to talk about real soon, then this must be important. I want to know who this lost son was, and what this sacrifice would be. What wrong we are righting. Add the fact that this came to you right when we're discussing the very idea of you going out there? Then we're going to do it."

"I don't think taking more than one person would be good. It might be a sign of aggression to the witches and anyone watching. Even though Valac is dead, we don't know who his master was, and the vampire attacks might have slowed, but they haven't stopped."

Chase nodded. "Meaning this is only the beginning. Someone is still out there. Someone killed the coven, someone was ruling Valac, and there will be more to come. More violence, more death, more blood. We'll fight against it, but you're right, I think you taking more than Cruz with you on this would be the wrong choice." He turned to Cruz, his gaze narrowed. "You are one of the strongest fighters out there. Protect her."

"She's not going to be hurt. Not on my watch."

"I can protect myself," I said.

"And I can help," Cruz growled.

We were openly snarling at each other. People stared between us, but they didn't ask questions.

That probably should have worried me, but I had so much on my mind just then, I couldn't focus on it.

"Wynter, I have a few things to go over with you to make sure that the wards are safe, plus all the spells and other healing additions that we've added to our repertoire since the attacks began."

"I'll help, don't worry. I'm off from my job for the next

two weeks, I get vacation." She rolled her eyes, and I frowned.

"What?"

Wynter waved us off. "It's a long story that I don't want to get into, but needless to say I might be looking for a new job." Hayes leaned forward, and I could see his bear shifter in his eyes.

"What do you mean? Tell us. Because you're trying to block your emotions and it's not working, little girl."

Wynter sighed and rubbed her hand over her heart. "It's fine, they weren't really excited with the fact that I was a human part of the Pack. I don't want to get into it right now because we have other things to deal with, but I'm here for the foreseeable future until I find another job to pay the bills. I will take over Dara's duties, except the actual magic parts, but I'm sure we have enough magic users within the alliance to help out. Now, I don't like being the center of attention so let's talk about the fact that Dara's going on a fricking road trip to go find power and witches and sounds a little bit scary. Let's talk about that."

I stared at my friend, and then at Wren who nodded tightly, and I had a feeling that we would be cornering her as soon as possible. Of course, it might just be Wren doing that because I was going on that road trip.

To find the power, to find my fellow witches.

I didn't know if we would rebuild the coven, or if we would find a way to stop the vampires and demon once for all.

It was only a first step.

A step that I would be taking with Cruz.

My power shifted as Cruz stared at me, and I knew that every step we took together without actually dealing with what we might have, it wouldn't be forever, it wouldn't be a potential mating.

No, it would be hate.

It would be an agony I didn't want to deal with.

I would focus instead on what I could handle.

A potential war, potential death, and everything else that came with my powers.

CHAPTER FOUR

Cruz

"Where are we going?" I asked as Dara frowned at her tablet.

"To the city. On the eastern edge, near Franklin Street. You'll know it when you see it."

I frowned, looking over at her for a moment before getting on the highway.

The Pacific Northwest Alliance had four main Packs in the area. We worked together, we fought together, and we protected one another. But there were also human cities and towns sprinkled within the territories. The den was part of our territory but it wasn't all of it. We were all very careful about whose territory was which, and it was

Steele's job, as well as mine, to work with our patrols to make sure that we were always keeping alert about who was entering our land. We had cameras and security for that, just like the humans, but they didn't always work with magic.

And it wasn't just magic from the vampires, but the witches too. The coven was no more, but as we were learning, there were numerous witches who had been forgotten by them long ago.

"So, how do you know these people?" I paused, trying not to sound so accusatory, but I couldn't help it.

Dara looked over at me, her lips twitching, before she outright laughed, but there was no humor in it.

"I know these people because while I have been a Pack member for a long time, I wasn't always. And even then, I didn't always live within the den. Blade made sure of that."

My hands fisted on the steering wheel when she mentioned our former Alpha. The man who had beaten us, hated us, and had used dark magic with witches that had threatened all of our lives. Not everybody had survived that purge, that hatred, and I swallowed the bile rising in my throat.

My mother hadn't survived Blade's torture. But she wasn't the only one, and it pained me even to think about it.

"I'm sorry. For bringing him up. I try not to do so around Chase, considering he's his son, or really anyone."

"We're all better off without him. That's just the truth."

"True, but I'm part of the Pack because of Blade, so I can thank him for that, at least."

I frowned, settling in with cruise control so I could listen to her.

"How is that? I was in and out of the den when you showed up, so I don't know the story."

Odd to think that I didn't really know the woman that had the potential to be my mate, but I might as well ask. We were stuck in a car together for a few hours until we reached the edge of the city, and I might as well use that time to make up for the lack of information.

"When Blade started to recruit witches, like the woman he eventually sacrificed, he brought a lot of us."

"Did he hurt you? More than using the powers through our bonds?" I asked, my voice low and fearful.

Dara shook her head. "No. He didn't really. The normal things that he did as a sadist, but you know that. None of us were left unscathed, even the ones we tried to protect the most." She huffed. "My parents were not harvester death witches, but they had dark powers. They weren't trained enough to even realize what they had, or use their powers in any way. They tried, but it wasn't enough. And when a rival coven came for us, my parents died protecting me."

I reached out and gripped her hand without thinking. We looked at each other, then down at the touch. I hadn't even expected to do that. I didn't want to let go, but I knew I couldn't hold her. Touch her.

She wasn't mine, and my wolf wasn't ready to lean into that need. So I let go, using the curve of the highway as an implied excuse.

"I lived on the streets from the time I was five until I was a teenager, when Blade found me. I had so much power that it bled from me, but I didn't know how to use it. I wasn't safe with the humans or in schools or in foster care. I couldn't hide myself, and we weren't exactly out with the humans then."

Humans knowing about witches and shifters was relatively new. We weren't sure—outside of some circles—whether they knew cat shifters and bear shifters even existed. This was all new for the world, hence why we were having so many battles and had to be so careful, when otherwise we would want to wipe the existence of vampires from the earth quickly. But if we did that, it would show our true natures, and the humans would chain us and cage us like they wanted to before. Or risk using the dark powers Blade used before, and we would send ourselves to our eternal damnation.

"How did you survive?" I asked.

"Thanks to the people we're meeting. Not all of them were nice, they were sometimes kind, sometimes not. Because they had to be. But we helped each other. Though we couldn't remain in one spot, not with the risks we each bring."

I stiffened. "Risks?"

"We're not meeting the elemental witches like you are so used to."

I turned to her for a second before I turned my eyes back on the road. "You're not an elemental witch."

"True. But I'm just the tip of the iceberg. I joined the Pack because I needed a home. Because I was dying without a connection."

I stiffened and glanced at her again. "What?"

"I'm a death witch. I need life to survive. The Pack bonds that bring us all together, that help you be stronger and faster and keep your den safe? I need those too."

"So you feed off of us?"

I knew I had said the wrong words as soon as they left my lips. Her face went ashen.

"I'm sorry. I didn't mean it like that."

"I don't feed off of you, but maybe I do. We all do. A Pack is symbiotic. Our Omega pulls in our emotions and tries to calm us when it's too much. The Enforcer uses our strength in order to protect us. The Healer uses power along the bonds in order to send life in. I don't take life, not in that way. But the connection to others helps feed my power so it doesn't drain me."

"You're saying without a Pack you were draining yourself." The true horror of that hit me as she nodded.

"Yes. And it was horrible. But I survived. And I felt I'd found a home, but I'd just found Blade."

"I'm sorry. But I'm not sorry that you're Pack." She snorted, and I shook my head. "What?"

"That was the nicest thing you've said to me in a while."

"I don't hate you, Dara."

"I know. I don't hate you either."

"But I'm killing you, aren't I?" My wolf howled, but I didn't back down. I couldn't. Not when Dara and I were finally talking. Yes, it took us being trapped in a damn car together, but it was the best we could do.

She cursed. "Cruz."

"No. You used too much power to bring me back, and that's why you're dying. Why you look exhausted, why it's worse since then, and it's not just because of the wards. It's me."

"You need to get off at exit seventy-four. Declan's an asshole, but he's kind too."

She wasn't subtle at all with her change of subject, but I let her get away with it. Mostly because I wasn't sure what I was supposed to say. Not when I knew it was the truth. Our Pack might be symbiotic, but I was parasitic.

"Declan?"

"He's an arrogant man, and a nice one."

There was something in her voice that set my wolf on edge, and I gripped the steering wheel tight enough that it creaked.

"Cruz," she snapped. "What's wrong?"

"How well do you know this Declan?" I asked, my voice a growl.

Out of the corner of my eye I saw her roll hers, as she went through her notes.

"I'm not a virgin, neither are you. And we're not mated. So get that tone out of your voice."

"So you slept with him. We're off to see your old boyfriend to try to help the Pack. Good to know."

"Shut up. We're off to see a man that I slept with a few times when we were both alone and exhausted and trying to figure out how to control our powers. He's a couple years older than me, and a damn strong witch. He's an asshole, but a good guy. And if I ask him for help, he'll come."

I didn't like the sound of that, didn't like the way that she sounded so sure of herself.

"Then what?"

"I can't call him, because he wards his phone so no one can find him." She paused. "He went against the coven, at least the leadership, when they were good at least."

"Are you kidding me? The coven that was actually our friends—he went against them? Are we trying to lead an enemy into our Pack? Because I feel like we've done enough of that recently."

We had already had more than one traitor within our midst, but that made sense. Our Pack had been broken, shattered beyond belief because of our Alpha, of course there would be more treachery within. But we were digging them all out, one traitor at a time.

"He went against them because he wanted to bring witches out into the public because he was tired of hiding. And it was not the right time."

"Interesting," I said, not sure if I actually meant that.

She laughed again, this time with a little more humor. "Well, the covens and myself didn't get a choice. And honestly, the former coven would've let him in, just like they did me, but I don't think he really wanted to be part of it. Not in the same way."

"And you think he wants to be part of it now?"

"I think we're all desperate, including him."

I hated the way she said his name, the way that my wolf wanted to reach out and bring her close, to mark her as mine.

She looked at me then, and I could scent her need.

Because there was no denying it. We had always wanted each other. But we never had one another. And now we were stuck in a car for who knew how long, and all I could do was scent her arousal.

"Stop looking at me like that."

"When you growl at me like that, and stare at me with those eyes of yours as they glow gold, what am I supposed to do?"

"Just stop."

She huffed out a breath and went back to her notes.

"What are you working on?"

"Declan I could find easily, as well as another one of my former friends, but I'm still looking for the others, and I'm working on spells for the vampires. Multitasking." She paused. "Thank you for driving."

"Thank you for not fighting with me about it."

She laughed then, and I smiled because it was genuine. The Dara that lay in the quiet places that others didn't see. "You're so dominant it's not like I really had a choice. And frankly, I don't like driving. I like being the passenger princess."

"What is that?" I asked, laughing.

"Oh, you know, the passenger who gets to take a nap and eat and play with the radio and just enjoy herself with a blankie and a pillow. What more do I need?"

"You're in leather pants, a leather jacket, and you're strapped to the nines with magical weapons in case we come across a vampire horde. No blanket in sight, just kick-ass power."

"I'm my own princess, thank you very much."

"Whatever you need."

She just shook her head, and thankfully things were quieter after that.

When we exited a couple of hours later, I followed her directions to a small, hipster area of town, with wrought iron fences and cheese stores and random florists everywhere.

"This is nice," I said, and I wasn't quite sure I was telling the truth.

Dara snorted. "This is a magical-hipster's dream."

"Oh?"

"All of these places cater to those with powers. Declan didn't make his own coven, but he did make a safe place for witches."

As we parked, I studied the area a little bit more. There were indeed a few florists, an herb shop, a tea shop, and a few cheese shops and butchers. None looked particularly magical, but I supposed you had to get your ingredients somewhere, which made me realize something.

"Where do you get your ingredients for your spells?"

She turned to me. "There's a local place that's much like this, that even humans who don't know what they're doing with their little fake spells use. And Declan ships me some from here. Overnight shipping is pretty amazing in this day and age."

I shook my head. "We're in the middle of fighting vampires, dealing with mates, and coming back from the dead, but at least you have overnight shipping."

"Well, I have needs." She sputtered as I narrowed my gaze, my wolf in my eyes. "I meant with supplies. We should get out of the car now. Declan knows we're here."

Those words felt like an ice-cold shower to me and I got out of the car, my senses on alert.

"He has his wards out so you're not going to be able to scent him, but that's his home."

"Yes, it is my home," a man with a deep voice, a Henley sweater, and shoulder-length honey-brown hair said as he walked down the stairs. I hadn't even realized he was there. "Dara, darling. You never visit anymore. But it seems you've brought a friend." Declan stared at me. "One that bites."

I grinned, showing all of my teeth. "Well, only if they ask nicely, and sometimes when they don't."

Dara looked between us and rolled her eyes. "You know what? Just whip them out and measure, because I'm just not in the mood for this. Declan, we need your help."

I held back a laugh at Dara's words, mostly because she sounded more like her feistier self than she had in ages. I just hated the fact that it had taken Declan to make that happen.

The male witch stared at her. "Why are you here, darling?"

She looked around at the people milling about. We weren't unnoticed, and I didn't like being out in public like this.

Declan seemed to sense our unease, because he nodded and gestured towards his home.

"Come inside, you will be safe here. I promise you."

Dara stepped forward, but I reached out and steadied her. "Dara?" I asked, a wealth of meaning in that one word.

"I trust him."

"That's good to hear, considering you left all of us."

She frowned. "Stop it, Declan."

"Just saying, darling. You'll be safe with me, wolf. I

promise not to poach, encroach, or anything else. You have my word as a witch."

I nodded tightly as Declan glared.

"Not going to say a witch's word isn't worth much?"

I shook my head. "I don't know about the chip on your shoulder, but I'm standing next to a witch I trust. So, what's your next dig?"

Dara shook her head and pulled out of my grip before walking past Declan. "It's urgent, we don't have time for this, Dec."

The other man sighed and followed her, and I did one last perusal of the street before making my way inside.

The place had dark furniture and dark stone-blue walls. It looked like Declan had done well for himself.

Dara whistled through her teeth as she studied the place. "Did you rob an older millionaire or something, Declan?"

The other man laughed. "No. I just happened to learn how to use stocks. Who knew? I can make my own money. Didn't have to live on the streets forever. You found your Pack, I found my own way."

I narrowed my eyes at him. "Did you?"

Declan laughed again, but this time it was a hollow sound. "Not a Pack, not a coven. But I found friends. People who needed help. I haven't stolen or cheated. I did what I was supposed to do—living the dream. Just with magic."

"Declan, we need your help. The Packs need your

help." She went on to explain about the wards, the witches, and the vampires.

Declan shook his head. "Vampires. Well, I still can't believe that's true. Though I shouldn't have been too surprised. Not with the atrocities we've seen."

"Declan, we need you. The Packs need you."

He glared at her, then at me. "And what have the Packs ever done for me? They never came for me, Dara. They plucked you right off the street to give you a home, and left me behind."

Dara glared. "And you know the man who took me, what he really wanted. You were safer in the end, so don't bring that up."

"Why are you here, Dara? After all this time. You have your precious coven. You don't need me."

He didn't know. The man really didn't know what had happened.

"The coven is dead, Declan," I growled.

The witch stared at me, then at Dara. "What?"

"Somebody infiltrated the coven, tore it apart, and killed them. I couldn't save them."

"Did you use your magic? Are you okay?"

I stared between them, wondering how she could have used her magic, but then I remembered—she was life and death. No wonder she had passed out right after trying to ease the burden. Because she was connected to both.

"I'm fine, but there's no one left. They pushed out those who weren't like them, and they were killed for it. I can't say I'm sorry to see some of them go, even if that makes me a horrible person, but they're dead, Declan. The vampires keep coming after us, and they're not going to stop with our Pack, our alliance. They're killing humans—pulling them off the streets, ripping their throats out and trying to start a war with the supernaturals. The witches are out now, you can't hide. We need you. We need to protect those that we couldn't before."

Declan looked at her, then at me. "And this wolf. Will he help us? Or just his Pack?"

My wolf pushed at me, we were damn tired of this man. "I'm her protector. I'll do whatever I have to."

Dara growled at me, and it just made me hotter for her. There was something wrong with me. "I can protect myself."

Declan looked between us and smiled. It looked genuine and intrigued. Wasn't quite sure how I felt about that.

He held out his hand and the metal cup he had been holding twisted before softening into a flat disk, and he tossed it into the drawer next to him.

I froze, not ever having seen that kind of metal magic before. I hadn't even known it existed.

"I'll join you. Because I'm tired of being the one who gets beaten because he's not the perfect elemental witch, and maybe the wolves could use me. After all, there's a lot more metal out there than ever. The world is my oyster, it's time they saw exactly what I can do."

Dara just shook her head, and I stared, wondering who else my mate had up her sleeve, and doing my best not to feel hope.

Hope that maybe we would find the strength we had been lacking.

Because if I had hope, we would only fail harder. That was how it always was.

CHAPTER FIVE

Cruz

I LOOKED DOWN AT MY PHONE, THEN OUT THE window at the setting sun before I turned to Dara.

"If we're going to get back out on the road and to our place to sleep for the night, we should be going."

We had been there for nearly an hour, and though I wasn't sure I trusted Declan, I was glad that Dara had been able to have this time with a fellow witch.

I had always known she had felt somewhat of an outsider. You couldn't stop that feeling. You couldn't hide it. But I hadn't known it had been that bad. I hadn't seen the lack of connection she felt until it was almost too late.

And I knew that was on me because I hadn't wanted to look too hard.

Her being around another witch, one who may understand her more than the elementals we knew and saw on a regular basis, had relaxed her, and while I hated the fact that this man, this ex of hers, seemed to be able to do that for her, part of me was just glad she had that option. That ability. And I needed to not be such a damn idiot about it.

It just wasn't easy to think about it like that. Not when all I wanted to do was ensure that she was safe. Happy.

Or at least that's what my wolf wanted.

It was hard to think about exactly what my wolf wanted these days because I was so used to ignoring him.

"You're right. We should go. We'll see you soon, Declan."

The man looked at me before he held out his arms and Dara hugged him close.

I didn't even realize I was growling until the sound echoed off the walls. The sight of them touching made me want to rip that other man's face off.

Dara raised a brow at me as Declan smirked and took a step back. He held up both hands and looked between us. "I figured. Sorry, old man. I'll refrain."

"Excuse me?" Dara bit out.

I lifted a lip, just showing a bit of fang. "Good."

"There's no *good* about this. We do not have time for this."

"You'll make time," I grumbled.

Her eyes narrowed to slits as I turned towards the window, the scent of something wrong hitting me far too hard.

And then I was moving, throwing myself over Dara before I even realized it.

Declan cursed, slamming his hands into the air. Metal shutters rang down, but it was too late for one of the windows as glass shattered inward, sliding towards us.

Jagged shards of glass sliced into my back as Dara pushed me out of the way, ignoring my shouts, and pushed her hand up into the air before making a fist and slamming it onto the ground.

She muttered something under her breath, and Declan cursed before the glass arrowed its way through the broken window and somebody screamed.

"I sure as hell hope that it was the person who put that bomb in front of my place and not an innocent bystander," Declan snapped.

"You know that spell. You taught it to me. It only went back to the sender."

"Well, that's good to know," I snarled before I stood up and shook off the debris. Blood seeped out of the open wounds on my back, but I ignored it. I didn't miss the way that Dara stared at me, eyes wide.

"You're bleeding."

"I'm fine."

"Blood is powerful, though. We can't just leave it here."

"On it," Declan said as he held out a match. "We'll burn it, as well as a few other things. Then we're going to see who dared attack my little abode."

"I knew something was off, we shouldn't have been out in the open for this long," I snarled.

"You think they're following us?"

"It's what I would do. But then again, I don't know who took Valac's place."

"Valac, that vampire general you killed?" Declan asked as he picked up a bag and kept moving. The scent of smoke hit the air as my blood burned, and I was grateful for it, since we were dealing with magic users here and blood was a very important element for them.

"Yes. He's dead, and we don't know who is next in line. But somebody is still organizing these vampires. Ruling them. And if they *did* follow us, then we brought them right to your doorstep."

Declan didn't look annoyed at that. If anything, he looked pleased.

"I've been waiting to meet these dumb idiots. They've taken a couple of my people in the past, and I'm not going to allow that to happen anymore."

I whirled on him. "What?"

"You really think the vampires are only focused on the Aspen Pack? They've been targeting magic users, too, the ones that are too weak to do anything. That's why I'm eager to help you. Not because I want revenge for the fucking coven that never wanted me in the first place. No, because they're killing witches. And I want it to stop."

I had questions, but now wasn't the time. Not when we needed to figure out who had done this. All I could scent were blood and debris.

We moved as one, and I had my focus on what was in front of us, as well as Dara. While Dara thought we needed Declan, he would be on his own for this. I didn't know him well enough to figure out how he fought.

We slid out of the front door, grateful that Declan used his magic to pull back these steel shutters.

That was a handy power, and I was going to be interested to see what the other Pack members thought of it.

When we made it out to the street, people were yelling and running up to Declan.

"It was a car, we're not sure who it was, but they threw some form of bomb toward you. More like a Molotov cocktail with vampire powers."

I turned towards the woman, who I sensed was a witch, and she smiled at me, though there was no humor in that gaze.

"I'm not a witch, but I can sense magic. In case you're wondering, wolf," the young woman snapped, and I just raised a brow, letting my wolf fill my gaze. She didn't back down, and I respected her for it, but I was exhausted and hurt, and my mate had almost been hurt and standing too close to a man that she had slept with before, and while we were all allowed to have pasts, I was a little too fucking territorial right then to care.

"Did they follow us, or were they already here for you?" Dara asked the question that had been whirling in my mind.

"I'm not sure, and this is where we split up, love."

"Watch it," I growled. I hadn't meant to say that, but there was no turning back now.

Dara stared at me wide-eyed before she shook her head, muttering something about men under her voice as she walked away.

"Fine, we'll meet you at the assigned place. Stay safe, Declan."

"Always." He winked at me before he went to the others to ensure they were safe.

The only damage seemed to be Declan's brownstone, though it worried me. I couldn't sense vampires around, but they had been here. They had been near us, and I was almost too late to deal with it. To help her.

To save her.

Before I could do anything about that though, Dara punched me in the shoulder. I looked down at her, lips raised in a snarl.

"What?" I asked, my voice cool.

"Get in the car. You're going to scare people if you don't stop."

"You could have died."

"And I didn't. You're the one bleeding. Still. And since

I don't want to clean you up here with everybody watching, let's go get your little hurt wolf into the car, and we'll get to the hotel. If they're following us, I want to know. If they were just here for Declan, I also want to know. We have to keep our Pack safe."

I wanted to reach down, pull at her ponytail, and crush my mouth to hers.

And because the wolf was running so high, it honestly didn't surprise me when I did just that. I wrapped her hair around my fist, pulled her head back, and pressed my mouth to hers. She tasted of smoke and wine, and I gorged on her, needing her.

She hummed into me, her nails digging into my arms as she held on tightly. And when someone whistled behind me, I ignored them for a bare instant, knowing I needed to keep my senses alert.

I couldn't sense danger, but that was only the beginning.

When I pulled away, I stared at her, eyes narrowed, panting.

"Mine."

She raised a brow.

"No. I'm not. But I know you're hurt, a literal wolf with a thorn in his paw right now. So let's get you someplace safe. And then we'll deal with whatever the hell just happened."

I glared at her, heart racing, but did as she asked.

Because she was my mate. And she was almost hurt. And I needed to do something about that.

Even if it went against everything I had already promised myself.

•

We ended up at a hotel over an hour away, one that we hadn't prepaid, so we were thankful to find a room there. It wasn't a hole in the wall place, it was more middle of the road. I didn't care where we slept, as long as I could keep an eye on her. Plus, Dara looked frazzled beyond normal exhaustion.

"Do you want to talk about it?" I asked.

She glared at me, before she threw her head back and laughed.

"I don't know what's funny about what just happened."

"Are you talking about the fact that we got our first ally? Or the fact that you were hurt? That vampires attacked us out of the blue? Or the fact that you kissed me in the middle of the street with everybody watching?"

"Honestly, any of that would be a good place to start."

She shook her head and I narrowed my eyes.

"You're standing there, chest heaving because your wolf is pushing at you. If we weren't in the middle of a damn city I would say you needed to shift so you could let your wolf breathe. But we can't do that."

She moved forward and I sucked in a breath, wondering what the hell I should do when she put her hand on my chest.

She looked so small next to me, so fragile.

"I'm okay. You are the one that got hurt. Not me."

"There's a bruise on your chin, and I bet one on your side where I slammed you into the ground."

She shook her head. "Maybe. But if you hadn't done that, I would've ended up with glass in my face, neck, and who knows where else."

A low growl escaped me as I prowled towards her.

"You are not calming me down right now by explaining to me how you could have been hurt worse."

"Well, I'm not calm either. You're still bleeding."

"I'm not bleeding. The wounds have closed up. Shifter healing."

She shook her head, hands outstretched. "Take off your shirt and let me see."

I quirked a brow and she narrowed her gaze.

"I don't have time to play games with you. I need to see that you're okay."

"I thought you weren't my mate. Why do you care?"

"Because I'm very good at lying to myself. You know damn well that we could be mates. You're the one who said it before. And I'm doing my best not to think about it, because I can't. You know I can't."

"And why can't you? Why haven't we?"

There it was, the question I told myself I would never ask.

"Because we're already connected. Because I brought you back when I shouldn't have, when the goddess told me not to. I changed everything. I don't know what would happen if we mated, what would happen to the connection that brought you back."

I cursed under my breath and cupped her face, needing that touch.

"Dara." I ground out the word, and she let out a shuddering breath, resting her forehead to my chin.

"I can't. But I need to. I don't know what I'm supposed to do."

"My wolf can't focus. Not with the scent of blood and smoke around you."

"Then let me see your wounds and make sure you're okay, and then you can check me."

I slid off my shirt, not knowing what else to do, as my wolf paced, needing more, and Dara slowly slid her hands over my body, down my chest, over my abs, and turned me around to look at my back.

"How is it?" I asked, my voice deep, guttural.

"You still have the marks, but you heal quickly."

She tapped her fingers along my side and I stiffened, sucking in a sharp breath.

"Ticklish?" she asked, her voice incredulous.

"I don't know, but I don't really want to find out right now."

She slid her hands down my side, and I willed my cock to behave. It pressed hard against my zipper, and I could barely breathe.

It was hard to do that when it came to her anyway.

"You saved me."

"You saved yourself."

"Your wolf, he's pacing. I can feel him."

"My shifter–I am two souls, one of wolf, one of man. Finding the balance between the two is what makes our dominance and our strength so important."

"So you're telling me it's not just the wolf pacing?" she asked. I sighed, and her warmth on my back was a touchstone I didn't know I needed.

"Pretty much."

"You're not the only one with warring magics inside."

I turned to her, needing to see her.

"What's wrong, Dara?"

"My magic, it needs life. And I hate it. I hate the fact that others think I bring death, that I can control it too, and yet all I feel is as though I'm the one running from it."

There was so much in that statement, so much trust in me for her to be able to say it out loud.

"What do you need, Dara?"

Her hands were on my chest as I tried to breathe.

"You. I need you."

I wanted to shout to the heavens, to scream and to mark her and claim her as mine, but we both knew that wouldn't happen. It couldn't. So I lowered my lips to hers and kissed her. Doing the one thing I knew I could, the one thing I knew I shouldn't. The one thing I knew I would crave until the end of my days.

"Tell me what you want. What you like. I need to know."

And not just because she was my mate.

I needed to stop thinking like that. To stop thinking that she was mine. Because she wasn't. She had put it plainly that she couldn't, and both of us had stepped away, but here she was, in my arms, so I would pretend. Because it was what I was good at.

I pretended that I belonged, that I knew where I came from, that I understood why I had become Heir.

So I would pretend that I knew why this was happening between us right now.

She didn't answer, instead she slid her hands up and down my chest, her skin cool to the touch along my heated flesh. When I kissed along her jaw, down her neck, she moaned for me.

It was a small hotel room, the king bed taking up most of the space, so it didn't take much effort to move her towards it. She slid her hands over her jacket, and I brushed her motions away, needing to undress her myself.

She stared at me, her eyes wide, her hair falling out of her ponytail.

"You're beautiful."

She still had the dark circles under her eyes, the wards

and whatever she had done to save me slowly leeching from her, but she was so damn beautiful.

And I would do whatever I could to heal her, to find a way to fix what had happened. I would not be her downfall, even though she was mine.

"You make my knees go weak, which I probably shouldn't say. I feel as if I say too much when I'm around you."

I snorted. "I never say the right things when I'm near you."

Her lips twitched, so I leaned down and gently bit down on the bottom one.

"What was that for?" she asked, her eyes wide.

"I can't help it. You make me crazy."

She opened her mouth to say something, but I couldn't focus, not with her right in front of me, so I kissed her again, this time sliding off her jacket completely, and then unbuttoning her shirt.

Her breasts were full, nearly overflowing her bra, and when I cupped them she groaned, her nipples hardening underneath my gaze. I slid my thumb over the lace, watching her nipples pebble into tight peaks.

"I need to taste them."

"Whatever you want."

I knew she had to be out of her mind if she was saying that, but I let myself believe it.

I leaned down and sucked one nipple into my mouth as she arched into me, moaning my name.

I would do whatever I could in my lifetime to earn that moan, my name sliding between her lips.

I continued to suck on her nipple, then moved to her other breast, before I was sliding her down to the bed, undoing her shoes, her pants.

She pulled at my pants, and then we were rolling around, fighting one another, our normal play that always felt as if it was our right, tearing at each other's clothes, finding each other naked, flesh to flesh, skin to skin.

I could barely breathe as I gripped her hips, pressing her against me. The hard length of my cock pressed against her belly and her eyes widened, looking between us.

"I won't mark you. But I'm a shifter, I can't get you sick, I can't get you pregnant. Not unless we're mated, not unless it's under the full moon."

She frowned. "Is the full moon still a thing? At least these days?"

I paused, groaning.

"You know, with the way matings have changed, maybe not. But I cannot get you pregnant unless we are mates."

That was always the rule, and it hadn't changed as far as I knew.

When she slid her hand over my cock and squeezed, my eyes crossed.

"And neither one of us can get diseases. So I want you inside me."

"I like it when you're forceful," I said with a rough chuckle.

"You're always the growly one. I'm just trying to keep up."

I smiled and slid my hand between her legs. She was already wet for me, the soft thatch of curls between her legs glistening with her arousal.

"So fucking beautiful," I whispered as I slid one finger and then another deep inside her. She groaned, her mouth parting in a little O, as I slowly breached her entrance and felt for that little bundle of nerves inside.

"Cruz," she muttered, her breath coming in pants.

"That's it. Say my name. Say my name as I fuck you with my fingers. And then I'm going to fuck you with my cock, and you're going to come on me, screaming my name."

"You have to make me come first," she whispered, and I grinned at the challenge, finding her spot and then using my thumb over her clit. She bucked against me, flying over the edge with just that one touch. I grinned, continuing to move my fingers in and out of her as she came down from her orgasm. And then, before I could think better of it, before I let myself stop and think about what this could mean, I slid her thigh up, spread her for me, and pushed inside her. The tip of my cock breached her, and she groaned, eyes wide as our gazes met. And then I moved, pounding my way, filling her quickly to the hilt.

She groaned, her pussy clenching around me as I moved slowly.

She was hot and tight and wet and mine.

No, not mine. I needed to remember that. She wasn't mine. And couldn't be. But I could pretend.

So we moved, arching into one another, her leg wrapped around mine, and we ended up with her on top, rolling her hips, my hands on her breasts, and then moving so she was beneath me, knees up practically to her shoulders as I pounded into her, both of us fighting for control, claws and fingernails digging into skin. I was gentle, as gentle as I could be between a shifter and witch, because she was far more fragile than me, not as strong, oh so breakable. But she was mine.

Mine.

And when she came again I let myself fall, knowing that her magic needed this, and my wolf did as well.

I took her mouth as I filled her with my seed, hips pumping as I continued to come, I knew that we were both lying.

That it wasn't just her powers, wasn't just my wolf.

No, the human halves of us needed this too.

The human halves who knew that we could never do this again. Not if we wanted to stay whole, to stay sane.

But I knew I would ignore that half of me.

Just for a taste of her.

The taste of my own damnation and the fate that was never meant to be.

CHAPTER SIX

Dara

Light slid through the blinds and danced along my skin and I opened my eyes, sore, emotionally torn, and wondered what the hell we had just done.

Cruz wasn't in bed. The light coming from underneath the bathroom door reinforced that fact. I hadn't even woken when he got out of bed, but maybe that was a good thing.

Because I didn't know what I was supposed to do. Not when everything hurt.

Yet, did it? Did everything truly hurt? I took stock of my situation and realized that the connection to Cruz, while still frayed, wasn't as painfully rigid as it usually was.

We did not have a mating bond. But when I had pulled him back from literal death, as a harvester witch, I had formed that line between our souls. I felt like a leech, and perhaps so did he, but with the essence of life and caring and whatever else we had had between us, perhaps it had helped. Perhaps the life aspect of my death magic had solidified.

Or maybe I was just trying to make something out of nothing because I was so worried about what had happened.

We had things to do today, things that had nothing to do with what we couldn't have.

When the bathroom door opened, Cruz walked out fully dressed, steam billowing out from the room, and he stared at me.

"You're awake."

His voice was low, gruff, and I swallowed hard. I sat up, grateful that I had put on his shirt the night before, chilled from the cold the thin walls couldn't keep out.

"I am. We need to meet Iris soon."

"Iris. She's the younger witch?" he asked as he moved to the small coffee maker and began to work with it. I sat up and stretched, knowing I was probably a little bruised from the night before, because even though he had been as gentle as possible, he was still a shifter, still a bit rough.

I had slept with shifters before. Like I told him, I

wasn't a virgin, but this had been different. Everything was always different with him.

And it had probably been a mistake, but I didn't have time to think about that. I wanted to do my best to just live in that moment, where I didn't have to think about the consequences, though it felt as if my entire existence was a consequence sometimes.

"She is a couple of years younger than me. I didn't really know her as well when I was living on the streets."

I didn't miss the way that he flinched as I said that, but there was no changing it. I had my past, just as he did. He hadn't always lived with the Aspens, even though he had always been Pack. He had been forced to live back in the den when his mother died, and Blade had forced everybody into seclusion soon after.

I didn't know how his life had been outside of the den, just like he only knew parts of mine. Perhaps the sharing was just one part of who mates could be. Though I knew we could never form that bond completely. I didn't know the consequences of that action. Would I lose him? Would he die?

And just like that, I was back on the battlefield, screams of terror ringing out as vampires came at us, one bite and blade at a time. The wards were failing, and my Alpha was on his knees, bloody, and moving towards his mate. Everybody was fighting as hard as they could, doing as much as they could, but I was so afraid it wouldn't be enough.

Because the vampires were using dark magic. Dark magic that we as healers and shifters and light magic users could never hope to fight against.

Because the darker the magic you practiced, the closer you went to losing your soul forever.

My magic wasn't dark. It was death, but death was an ending, a part of existence. It was natural. And dark magic wasn't. And that was what people didn't understand.

As vampires came at us, I had held my hands out, bleeding and broken, trying to keep our innocents safe by keeping the wards up. But it wasn't going to be enough.

And then Cruz was in front of me, eyes wide as a vampire took his sword and sliced it through Cruz's chest. It was just one instant, one motion that I could barely comprehend. Because that was supposed to be me. The vampire had come after me.

But he had taken the blade instead.

And then it felt as if the world shattered, one gasping breath, and I screamed.

The earth shook, waters raged miles away, and fire bloomed wherever it sparked.

That wasn't my magic, but in death and life I was connected to all.

I threw up my hands, the wards pulsing, as I went to my knees. Hayes, another shifter and our Omega, nearly collapsed at the pain of what had just occurred.

Because Cruz lay before me, eyes unseeing, mouth parted in a silent scream.

I was too late. I was going to be too late.

And the Omega knew it. Chase staggered and I knew our Alpha would know it soon.

I'd only a few moments to do this, to betray my goddess and do everything I knew I wasn't supposed to.

I'd knelt and put my hand over his chest.

I ripped into my magic. I didn't have time to center myself or calm my nerves. There was no ritual or candles or anything that would aid me. I wasn't a pure-born witch who knew what she was doing intuitively. Instead I was screaming, begging. I closed my eyes and sent myself down through the power that was my magic.

He was there. I could feel him, fading away, but I could catch him. It was as if it were a spiderweb of light and darkness and I dove between the threads not touching any of them. For they were the light and the darkness and the lifeblood of our Pack. I maneuvered between them, as if I'd been doing this all of my life, even though this was so taboo I had never even thought to try before.

I saw him falling, arms outstretched, eyes wide.

"Dara," he whispered.

Blood poured from his mouth, from his chest—he was gone. This was just the jagged part of his soul that still remembered who he had been.

I didn't know what lay on the other side, but I knew he couldn't go there yet. This was not his time.

He would not die for me.

I moved quickly, reached for his hand, and grasped it.

In that instant, things were right, wrong, and everything in between. I screamed, glass shattering around us as the world knew its maker.

For it was not me, it was not Cruz, but it was the one who made us all.

The goddess screamed with me, and I knew she would hate me, but there had been no choice.

He looked at me, eyes narrowing, and I smiled a sad smile. Because if this didn't work, he wouldn't be the only one lost today.

"Come with me."

"Dara? Are you hurt? Why are you bleeding?"

I looked down, saw the same bloody marks on my chest that were on his.

"We need to go now."

"Not if you're bleeding. Come on, we need to save you. Dara. Baby."

Tears slid down my cheeks. Because here he was sweetness. He was life. He loved me. Though he didn't know it, and he never would. Because if I did this, I knew the mating bond could never come. This would take place of it, to save him I would lose him. And I would do it over and over again.

"Please, Cruz. Come with me."

"Anything for you. Just stop crying."

"Of course. Come now. Let me protect you."

"I thought that was my job."

"You can do that soon. I promise."

And I had to hope I wasn't lying.

And so I pulled, screaming as I brought him back.

And it was over.

And he would never remember.

But I would. I always would.

"Dara. Wake up. Dara. What's wrong?"

I blinked and looked up at him, shaking my head. "I'm sorry. What just happened?"

"You were staring up into space. What the hell, baby?"

I shook myself and pulled away from him. I couldn't have him touch me, not when he didn't remember. Not when I couldn't let him.

Hurt crossed over his features for a bare instant before he steeled himself and nodded tightly.

"You're awake now? We need to go soon."

"I'm sorry. I didn't mean to zone out like that."

"It was more than zoning out, we both know it. But if you're not ready to tell me, I'm not going to force you."

Tears threatened again, but it was fine. It was better this way. It had to be. Because it hurt too much to think about what would happen if I let him know. If I let him see.

I was dying. I knew it. Unless we found a way to fortify our power base, and to stop the magic leeching from me to keep him alive, it would be the end.

And so I just wouldn't think about it.

"Let me shower quickly, and then we'll meet Iris."

"I'll get us something to eat. And then will you tell me more about Iris?"

I nodded. "Of course. I'll be sure to tell you about each of the witches in the future. I'm so used to keeping them secret, that I feel like I kept you off kilter with Declan."

His jaw tightened at the mention of Declan, so I told myself I wouldn't mention him again.

I showered quickly, and let my hair air dry around me, using the bit of glamour that I had to fix it. It wasn't much, but I didn't want to show up to Iris's looking weak.

"You ready to go?" he asked, studying my face. Perhaps he wanted to see more than was there, but I didn't have anything else to give.

•

Soon we were in the car, on our way to Iris's place. It had been a couple of years since I had seen her, since Iris and I didn't always get along. But that wasn't a prerequisite to us working together. She was sweet sometimes, and sometimes she couldn't be. But that was because of her magic. And when I explained this to Cruz, he growled low under his breath.

"What?"

"Are you sure she will help us?"

"I think she might." I let out a breath. "Her magic is with auras."

He frowned as he turned down the street, his wolf in his gaze. "I don't know what that means."

"Every being on this earth has an aura. It is part of their soul, and who they are as a person on this plane, just on the spiritual plane." I waited for him to cough or do something else, but he just nodded. "I was expecting you to comment about that."

"I'm a shifter who can change my body into something that doesn't have the same mass as my current one. I am friends with literal spirit witches, and last night I slept with a harvester death witch. I don't think me believing in auras is a leap here."

I just shook my head, glossing right over that because I didn't have the emotional wherewithal to deal with it.

"Well, she can, I don't want to say mess with, but she can alter auras."

He parked on a side street, turned off the car, and stared at me. "Okay, now I want to know what that means."

I shook my head. "I don't know exactly everything, and it can be a good thing or a bad thing."

"What does she do?"

"It's along the lines of an Omega. If your aura is to the point that it's damaged, she can help." I paused. "Or she can do the exact opposite. I've only seen her do that once though, and it was to someone who was trying to hurt us. I don't think she uses it as a weapon if she can help it, but it's a possibility."

He glanced at me. "I won't let her hurt you."

I sighed. "You're the one I'd be more worried about. She can't hurt me. My magic is stronger."

"And my fangs and claws can be used to protect or damage. So I guess we're all on the gray side of morals sometimes."

"You are good. You protect everyone that you can. Don't call yourself gray."

I hadn't meant to say that out loud, and when he looked back at me, I sighed and got out of the car. Thankfully, he followed and didn't ask about it.

"How close is she?" he asked, and I was grateful for the change in topic.

I pointed towards the small house at the end of the road. "She's there. And she knows we're here. I can feel her wards."

"I can feel something, but not what they are. That's a neat trick."

I frowned, tapping my chin. "I can probably come up with something."

"What do you mean?"

"I don't know. Something for you to sense wards like I do? I don't know if it would work with every shifter because you all have your own sense of magics and things, but with the way that, well..." I let my voice trail off, and he nodded in understanding.

"Any help would be appreciated. And I can still teach you self-defense."

He winked as he said it, reminding me of a conversation we had when we first met. I had tripped trying to just walk down the path. It was because I had seen him and my magic had yearned for him. But he didn't need to know that. He had jokingly offered to help me learn how to walk correctly, and we had started fighting from that moment on.

It was just so hard to focus when he was around.

"Get out of the cold," Iris said from her porch. "I've made tea."

I smiled at the redheaded witch as she winked at me. Then her hair turned a bright purple, then a bright blue, and I laughed.

"Really?"

"I'm trying out a new hairstyle. I'll make it permanent one day without a glamour, but it's all a frizz right now with my mood."

She waved at Cruz beside me. "Well, you're cute. Dara did well for herself."

I stiffened, and then I realized that she could read exactly what I was feeling. The confliction, the connection, the fact that I wanted him and hated him all at once. Oh good, there was never hiding anything from Iris, and that was one reason why we didn't spend much time together.

"Iris?"

"Yes, and you are?" she asked, pointing to Cruz as we walked inside. The wards slid over my body, and I was grateful for them. Because they were protection, and they were welcoming. And they weren't trying to leech any magic from me or Cruz.

"I'm Cruz. What magic did I just walk through? I only did so because I trust Dara."

Iris smiled wide. "That's a good idea. And they're just protection wards from outsiders. Since you told me you were coming, I keyed them to open for you guys. Don't worry. I'm not trying to take your magic. Or change your auras. I'm just trying to live my life."

"It's good to see you, Iris."

The younger woman smiled, her hair raven black now. "It's good to see you too. I've missed you. You look tired, Dara. Let's get you that tea. And some bread and cheese and meat. You'll eat, store up some energy, and maybe we can talk about the fact that your magic is weakening right in front of me."

I shook my head quickly as Cruz cursed under his breath.

"Dara," he grumbled.

"It's fine."

"From what I can tell, your aura got a boost last night. I won't pry too much, however, something's wrong, darling. You know that."

"I do. But we have other things to worry about."

"The coven?" she asked as she began quick work with a small meal.

"I told you part of it over the phone."

"And Declan told me the rest." She shrugged as she said it, and I cursed.

"I'm sorry I didn't tell you."

"It's okay. You're trying to contact us all. I just don't know how my magic could help."

"I can sense your power, and it's a lot," Cruz said as he nodded. "And thanks for the cup of tea." He handed it directly to me, and took the second one from Iris. Iris didn't miss the motion, and raised a brow at me. I just glared at her, and her lips twitched.

Oh, she could read the tension in our auras, I didn't even have to blush in front of her. Lovely.

"I have some strength, Dara is stronger than any of us."

"I don't know about that."

"You are. You always have been. Even though you had to hide it sometimes. If the coven's really gone, do you want to build a new one?"

"I don't think it's a want. I think we need a collective body to help."

"The coven didn't help us before," Iris spat, then held up her hand. "I'm sorry. That was rude."

"It was the truth. But whatever the coven turned into? It's not what they started as. They were a bunch of fucking idiots, and though they're dead, and I regret the loss of life, they hurt all of you. So fuck it. Build what you need to. However, it's not just the witches that need help."

Iris stared at him, then at me, before she smiled wide. "I like him. And I need to think." She held up her hand before we could speak. "It's a bit to ask. I'm good on my own. I'm hidden. From the vampires, from other witches who want to use me. I've always been hidden. But I understand duty. So give me a moment or two to think. I can meet you soon if you want. Maybe for dinner? I know that's not kind of me to ask, but it's changing my life. I want to make sure that I can do it. My magic takes a toll, as you well know. And I want to make sure that I won't be a risk."

I nodded, set down my tea, and hugged her tightly.

"Then let's eat for a moment, while I prepare to go see the others."

"Who are you seeing next?" Iris asked, her eyes filled with laughter as we sat back down.

"Jade," I said. Iris threw her head back and laughed, Cruz looking between us.

"What am I missing here?"

"Jade is amazing. She is kick-ass, and could probably take you down." She paused. "Okay, maybe not you, but another wolf. How long has it been since you've seen her?"

I grimaced. "More than a year." I looked over at Cruz. "Jade was my best friend on the streets. She's still a good friend. She's just been out of the country, traveling as much as possible trying to help others. In a way, she's been a mobile coven of one. But now I have to ask her to settle down and help me."

"Will she do it?"

"I wouldn't ask her if she wouldn't. But she hasn't

really accepted the decision I made."

Cruz cursed under his breath, and Iris winced.

"Ah. I wasn't going to mention it."

I shook my head. "And don't. We're dealing."

Cruz just snorted, and I sipped my tea. "We will deal."

"So, Declan, Jade, and me? Anyone else?"

"Leta and Bishop. I hope they'll work out."

Iris frowned and nodded. "Bishop will be the quiet one. He's an asshole but might help. I don't know though, are you sure bringing Cruz with you to see him is a good idea?"

I answered Cruz's question before he even asked. "Bishop doesn't like wolves. I don't know why, but he doesn't."

Cruz leaned forward, his wolf in his eyes. He was of both natures, there was no denying that. He couldn't hide it and I wouldn't want him to. "And you want to ask him to help the Packs?"

"He has a good heart. I think it's important to ask, because the coven shunned him. So he needs a home too. And we don't always have to agree."

"And who is Leta?"

Iris smiled softly. "A lovely woman. And I love her. It would be good for her to find a home. She's been lost for so long."

My heart ached and I nodded tightly.

"I think she'll help. I think she's just been waiting for

that home, and I want to make sure she has it." I turned to Cruz. "Leta is older. I think around seventy? And she's never been part of a coven, and only on the periphery of some of us. I want her to feel at home. I want to make sure that she knows that she's not alone."

Cruz nodded. "Meaning if she says no to the coven, you still want to help her. Okay. I can do that."

Iris's eyes widened as she looked between us, then at our auras, but I shook my head a fraction. I didn't want to know, I couldn't.

We said our goodbyes, planning when we would meet again.

"She's nice. I didn't know what I was expecting."

"She's innocent in some ways, hardened in others. I really like her. Hell, I like everyone that I'm asking. And hopefully we can find more witches that will help us defeat vampires."

"They need a home. A den. A Pack. I get it. I'm not a lone wolf, I need a Pack too."

We turned the corner to our car, when I staggered, magic slashing at me.

My eyes widened, and I turned to run, Cruz beating me to Iris's door.

The door was on its hinges, the wards broken. I screamed, terror radiating through me.

"Dara, don't."

"No. No!"

I went to my knees, tears sliding down my cheeks as I

touched Iris's face, hating what I had done, hating that I couldn't bring her back. We had been gone not even five minutes. And I hadn't been quick enough.

Iris lay on the ground, a pool of blood growing its macabre art around her, as her eyes stared at me vacant, wide-eyed.

Her hair, an ashen brown, no longer carrying glamour.

Whoever had come in had been quick and slit her throat with one precise movement.

I pressed my hand to her chest, trying to make sure she was sent on the right path, and I staggered, because somehow this was Iris and it wasn't.

"They siphoned her magic, Cruz," I gasped, my hands shaking. My own magic pulsed, confused, wanting to help. Only there was no help to provide.

"We need to go, darling." His voice sounded distant, as if he wasn't even aware of what he was saying. Then again, him calling me darling meant perhaps we were both in shock. "I called the Pack, they'll send someone to clean this up. To protect her. But we need to go. I don't sense anyone here, but that's not saying much considering what's happened the past two times we've met your friends. Not with whoever might be on our tail."

I looked at him then, and I knew. Someone was following us. Was trying to kill us. And they had killed Iris instead. I lowered my head, weeping, but not with grief, nor sadness. But with anger. I would destroy those who had done this. If it was the last thing I did.

CHAPTER SEVEN

Lily

Lily ran her hands through her hair, loving the way that the waves started to make their appearance. She had spent years straightening her hair, making it look soft yet flat. Hiding herself because that's who he needed her to be. But now her hair could use its natural wave, voluptuous, sexy.

Lily was the future, and all those Pack members who didn't think she had any power would weep once they met the real her. They didn't understand the power that she held. But they would.

She grinned and slid her bra back on, making sure her breasts looked pert, perky, and as high as possible. She didn't have large breasts, a bit more than a handful, and her consort loved them. She didn't need anything else. He had been here for so long, living amongst the humans, that they hadn't even realized that his power was there waiting, but Lily had. Lily always had.

Now she had to take her next step—what her consort desired and what she had planned.

The vampires were only the first step. They hadn't even realized they had been cannon fodder.

It annoyed her that Valac had failed so miserably. Not surprising though, because he had been so focused on Sunny, and hadn't realized what he could lose. The damn man was his own failure, and she was just happy that she didn't need to deal with his whining anymore. She'd had to pretend she was weak in front of him, a weak little human who wanted to be a witch that didn't have enough power to light a single flame.

Lily slid on her tank top, then her leather jacket, then snapped her fingers together, grinning at the flame in her palm.

"Who's powerless now?" she murmured.

Because Valac and Sunny were dead. Killed by the Aspen Pack. Or was it the Centrals? She didn't know anymore. It was hard to remember all of the animals and what they called themselves.

They had never wanted her, never thought her worth them.

Well, fuck them. Fuck all of their little powers and

what they thought was important. Because they would never have it.

She was the power. The future.

Lily giggled, slid her black boots on, strapped the leather buckles down, and made her way into the front foyer.

Her master had bought her this townhome months ago, when she was still pretending to be a weak little witch who couldn't use her powers to do anything. It had been their place to fuck, to need, and to grow her powers.

She held the blood of her enemy in her hand because of her master. Her consort.

Malphas was a true demon and power. And soon the witches and shifters and humans would bow before him, with her at his side.

She fluffed out her hair, and was grateful she hadn't put on makeup. At least a small glamour though so she looked sweet and innocent, so the man in the other room would do what she needed.

She grinned, the power thrumming through her.

Malphas had taught her how to siphon magic off others, and when she licked the blood of those witches into her mouth and swallowed their essence, she became stronger. She had taken what was her due.

The coven was no more, but in essence, they had never been important. They'd only been the steppingstone. She had put them in power, and then had taken it away because she didn't need them anymore. She had needed to break the Pack's confidence, and then break the Pack. The coven was worthless after that.

Well, the strength that came from those who died was worth something, but that didn't matter. She was a consort witch. A witch with multiple powers. And no one could take that away from her.

She did her best not to smile, to not look too brilliant. Because if she did, the human on the other side of that door would know. And he needed to think she was sweet, and dumb, and she needed help.

She wore a tattered brown leather jacket, one that made her look as if she needed help, that she had tried to fight and hadn't made it through whole.

She knew what she needed to do. She always had.

"Miss Morningstar," Matthew said as Lily walked into the room, her eyes wide, her lips bruised from biting into them. She tried not to smile at the name. It might be a little too on the nose to use that as her fake name. But her first name was actually Lilith, the mother of hell in some ideologies. She might as well use Morningstar to get what she wanted. Malphas loved it when she told him, and then he had taken her to bed, and marked and claimed her as his. She had come multiple times that night and had fed on his power, becoming more powerful with each stroke.

She pushed those thoughts from her mind\ though, because they weren't important right now. They couldn't be.

"Matthew. Thank you for coming. I've just been so worried."

He took her hands in his big, beefy ones that encompassed hers, and she leaned into him, a small waif who needed help.

"How can I help you, dearest Lily."

"It's been so horrible. They keep attacking us, and I don't know how to keep my friends safe. You know who I mean. Those of us who really know."

Matthew nodded. "We at Humans Only Group understand. And we will always be here to protect those who need us."

Lily resisted the urge to roll her eyes at the fact that Humans Only Group had the acronym HOG. But she didn't let it show.

He was ignorant, an idiot, and hateful. And he was exactly what she needed.

"The witches and wolves are killing us. Please, help us."

She put as much pitifulness and helplessness into her voice as possible, and he nodded, cupping her face. Lily resisted the urge to move away, but she did what she had to. It was what Malphas wanted.

"Anything for you, Lily. Tell us what you need, and my boys will be on it."

Lily grinned, knowing her next step. Knowing that little Dara thought she had the upper hand, but she didn't.

"You helped so much already, with the one who was

putting those bad spells on me. But she's gone now. And now I have another name for you. And this one is horrible. Worse than anyone else. Please help."

He cupped her face as she told him her plans, knowing that her consort was watching from the shadows. As he must, until it was time to show his face to the world.

And their plans could truly come to fruition.

Humans Only Group, HOG, might be a terrible name, but they had the firepower to make this happen.

After all, Lily could only have so much blood on her hands. It took forever to get out of linen.

CHAPTER EIGHT

Dara

"We should be there soon." I squeezed my hands into fists trying to calm myself, though there was no calm to come.

"Did you talk with Declan?" Cruz asked from the driver's seat as he turned down the next street.

I nodded, though I knew he couldn't see me with his eyes on the road in this pouring rain. It wasn't storming too badly, and with a wolf's keen eyesight, I wasn't afraid with him as a driver, but I knew the fear roiling within me had nothing to do with him. Or perhaps some of it did, but the majority of it was for what was to come.

Iris was dead. Gone. She was so sweet, had a future,

and they had taken her life without a second thought. Taken her magic before I had even had a chance to help.

I knew it wasn't a coincidence that we had been attacked at Declan's too.

Were we leading these monsters to my friends? Or were they already under surveillance?

And that was the problem. Because powerful witches like my friends were always being hunted. It was why we tried to hide. It was why I had tried to find safety within the Aspen Pack to begin with, to hide from other humans, the governments, other witches, other paranormals. They wanted my power, or what they thought it was, so I hid, just like my friends had.

I had been successful, at least in a way.

But now Iris was dead.

Cruz's hand touched my knee, and I froze before turning to him. "Dara. Focus."

I let out a breath. "Sorry. I was just thinking."

"I know. I know. Steele is on his way. Other wolves that are closer to the area are coming too. They're protecting Iris's legacy. They're keeping the human authorities away. It's the only thing we can do right now."

"I know. Thank you."

"What about Declan, did you call him when I was on the phone with the others?"

"Yes. Sorry. I nodded, but I guess you didn't see."

"I saw. But I needed you to say it. I needed you to speak. I just need you. Okay?"

I flinched. I didn't mean to, but I did. But he still squeezed my knee again, and didn't let go. I put my hand over his, and squeezed back.

We couldn't complete the mating, I knew that. And this was too close to caring, which would only make things harder in the end. Because he couldn't be mine, not when it could kill us both. But I just wanted to pretend. Even if it was one of the stupidest things I could do.

"Declan's okay?"

"He's fine. He's with others, and he's making sure that nobody can find him or those who rely on him. He's good at hiding."

Cruz muttered under his breath.

I snorted. "Declan and I haven't been together in a long time. He was only a friend that I needed back then."

"Not any of my business."

That made me laugh, surprising myself. Because I didn't think I could laugh, not after everything that had happened.

"I think you most of all are allowed to be growly. Because I know wolves. You get territorial even when you shouldn't."

"You're a witch. You don't get territorial at all?" he asked.

"I wouldn't say that."

Because I had seen him.

"What are we going to do?" I asked after a moment, trying to collect my thoughts.

"We're going to get to this Jade person's house, try to keep all of us safe, and perhaps get us home. Because my wolf and I cannot stand the fact that you're in danger."

I looked at him right as we parked. "Are you serious? I'm always in danger. We're in a war, Cruz."

"That's not helping my wolf."

"I don't know how to soothe your wolf. Not when we're both trying to figure out how to fight these things. Vampires are coming after us. And something learned how to siphon the magic from Iris. Something that tasted familiar."

"Like with the coven?"

I nodded tightly. "Yes. And I don't know what that means." He turned off the car and stared at me. I shook my head and sighed. "We need to find Jade."

"And then I need to get you home."

"We still have two more."

"Other people can find them. Hell, send Declan out."

"Declan doesn't know them as well as I do. I can help. Let me do this."

I got out of the car, slamming the car door behind me. I had put on a muting spell so that way nobody could overhear us. That was something I was decent at, though not the greatest. I hadn't done it before because it took energy, but I knew Jade would have food and other ways for me to restore my energy. She had been my closest friend, before everything had gone to hell and she had been forced to hide. And I trusted her.

I just hated the idea that I wasn't able to take her with me, because even when the Aspens had not been good—when the former Alpha had hurt us—I had still been in a better situation than Jade.

I walked towards the alley where I would find the wards for Jade's home. Cruz followed closely, his feet silent, but his presence always there.

The bond between us that wasn't of mating, but of death and choice, pulsed, and I held back a shiver.

"Don't walk away right now. We need to finish this."

I whirled on him. "Finish what? Iris is dead. Either someone knows where the witches are, or they're following us. We killed Iris."

"No. You don't get to put that on yourself."

"You don't get to tell me what to do."

He put his hand around the back of my neck, claiming me. I hated that I wanted to lean into him, wanted more, so I just stood there, frozen in place.

"Don't do this, Cruz."

"Don't do what? Comfort you? Your friend is gone, and I'm sorry for that. But that was not your fault. The monsters who are trying to hurt us all are responsible. We're going to figure out who it was, and end them. We're going to save your friends, and we're going to remember Iris. But you going off half-cocked and wanting to hurt somebody in retribution, to the point that you're not thinking clearly, isn't going to help anyone."

I fisted my hands and licked my lips. His gaze followed

the action, and I hated myself for wanting more. That was always the case with Cruz, though.

"Talk to me."

"There's nothing to talk about."

"I'm not going to let anyone hurt you, Dara."

"Why can't you be mine?" I asked. I hadn't meant the words to break free.

Cruz let out a soft growl, one that went straight to my toes, my core, and then his mouth was on mine, and I was kissing him, unable to hold back.

"I need you to be okay," he growled against my lips. Before I could say anything in response, he crushed me to him, and I clung right back. My fingers dug into his leather jacket, his hands around my hip, the others sliding into my hair as he adjusted my head so he could kiss deeper. I knew I was making a sound, moaning or groaning or doing something, but I didn't care. I just needed him.

Even if he was my worst intoxicant, my worst drug. But I was addicted, and I always had been.

I was the dealer of death, the harvester of souls, and yet the only thing I needed to thrive was Cruz.

Somebody cleared their throat behind me and I stiffened. Cruz pushed me behind him, growling low. His eyes were glowing gold, and the only way I knew was the way it reflected off the light pole next to us. His chest heaved, and I knew my lips were swollen, my hair a mess. I could barely breathe, barely hold back.

My pulse raced, and it was hard to even think with the

sound of my heartbeat in my ears, but then I heard a very familiar voice.

"You do realize we could hear you right? Your spell works against most, but not against me. Because that's the spell I taught you, Dara. Now, what exactly are you doing with this wolf near my home? And so loudly."

"Dara," Cruz asked low, just for my ears.

My lips, swollen, greedy for Cruz, quirked into a smile as I patted his back.

"It's okay. This is who we came for." I ducked underneath his arm before he had a chance to scold me not to.

I scented Jade's magic before I could see her, and then she smiled at me and threw open her arms.

I wrapped my own arms around her, holding her close, as her familiar fiery magic enveloped me, soothing my soul in a way that I hadn't thought possible.

It had been over a year since we had seen each other, and even then it had only been for a brief moment. We had both been fighting our own battles, dealing with our own messes. I hadn't seen my best friend in so long it hurt.

Yes, I had Audrey, Skye, Adalyn, Wren, Wynter, and Novah. They were my dearest of friends. Just like Lily had been, before we lost her. But Jade had been the friend of my youth.

Her long red hair was tied back in a braid, loosely done as if she had just tied it back from her face as she had worked. When I pulled back to stare at her face, her bright blue eyes were full of mischief, but I knew that was just a mask. She had to be as worried as I was.

"You're looking a little scattered."

"Did you hear?" I asked softly.

Jade pushed my hair back from my face, such a motherly gesture even though we were the same age.

"I've heard. I'm so sorry, darling. I'm so sorry for all of us. Let's get you and your very fine wolf back into my home beneath my wards. You went through the first set of wards, ones that I keyed to you and those you bring with you, but they're not enough."

"Okay. Let's go."

I pulled away and turned to Cruz, who was just staring at me with a raised eyebrow.

I cleared my throat.

"Here is who we've been looking for. Cruz, Jade. Jade, Cruz."

"I would ask if he was your mate, but that's not the bond that I feel." Sadness reached her eyes before she blinked it away and turned to Cruz. "Well met, wolf. Come inside. You must be hungry after your journey."

"Well met," Cruz growled. "But is there a reason you're sounding as if you're in some play about witches instead of in a metropolitan city?"

Jade grinned at him, shook her head. "I always like sounding like a mysterious witch. It helps with the aura. But come in. Sawyer's waiting."

"Sawyer's here?" I asked, brows raised. I didn't know him well, but I knew Jade trusted him.

"Who the fuck is Sawyer?" Cruz asked, as he was suddenly by my side, protective stance in evidence.

"Sawyer is a human. A friend. Nothing more."

I raised a brow.

Jade's eyes narrowed before she laughed. "Seriously. Sawyer is not mine. He's a friend. And we protect each other. It's what we do when there's forces out to get us."

"What forces are out to get him?" Cruz asked, distrust in his tone, and frankly I didn't disagree with him. Someone was after us, and I didn't know Sawyer. We had met once in passing. He wasn't from our past, but if Jade trusted him then maybe I should too.

A man with dark black hair and bright green eyes stood in the doorway to greet us.

"I'm no worries for you. I don't plan on hurting you, or your Pack. I would say well met, but it seems Jade here already tried the mysterious look and it didn't work. Come inside behind the wards. I'm human, so passing through them burns a bit. I'd rather not do that."

I turned to Jade who nodded, before she walked through the wards herself. Sawyer looked between us and gestured for us to walk through. I wanted to reach out and grip Cruz's hand, to find comfort, but I didn't want to rely on that. I couldn't rely on that.

Instead, he moved past me, touching his hand to the wards before he nodded tightly and looked behind me.

"Go through, before anyone finds us."

"Okay," I whispered, exhaustion settling in.

I moved through the wards, familiar yet painful. Jade didn't use subtlety when it came to them. If she didn't want you in, you didn't come in, but it still hurt. That was her magic, fiery and jagged, just like mine was dark and smoky.

Cruz let out a slight growl as he moved through, his eyes glowing gold, and I did the one thing I told myself not to. I reached out and gripped his hand.

"It's okay."

"Not a nice and familiar welcome there."

"Your wards aren't any more familiar to me. Remember that, wolf."

There was something in her tone that I didn't like—the way that she snapped back at Cruz so quickly even though she didn't know him.

"What's wrong?" I asked, and she shook her head.

"Nothing, other than the usual. People are trying to kill us, and here we are, about to have tea so you can actually get some rest. What are you doing to yourself, girl? You're far too tired, far too skinny. Why haven't you been taking care of her, wolf?" Jade asked, glaring daggers at Cruz.

"You try telling Dara what to do. I would love to see it."

"Don't gang up on me. I'm fine."

The way that I swayed slightly belied the lie. Cruz

growled, deep and low in his throat, which sent shivers through me, and suddenly he had his arms around me and was picking me up.

I pushed at his shoulder.

"Stop it. I'm not weak."

"You're not weak, you're just stupid right now."

Sawyer whispered something under his breath that made Jade laugh.

"No, I don't think they're mated. However, there is something there."

"It's not nice to talk about people when they're in the room in front of you," I grumbled as Cruz set me down on the couch.

"True. Now, let's break bread and eat some soup."

"Again with the witch-of-mystery tone?" I asked.

"I'm literally going to break the bread, and then slice it. But yes, I'm trying to act all supernatural and powerful in front of your friend here. The Heir of the Aspen Pack in my home. I should be honored."

Cruz narrowed his gaze between us. "I should ask what that means, but maybe I don't want to know."

"It means I know what the Pack has done in the past. But now they seem to be on the right track, which is good for Dara here. But I want to know why you're pulling us together like this."

"I had to come to you, so you could see my magic, because this can't be done over the phone. We need you.

And it's not just the Packs that need you. Witches need you. The coven that we could make, needs you."

Jade pressed her lips together. "The coven has never wanted us."

"The coven is dead."

Jade nodded. "I know. People whisper. And I know you wanted to be here to ask me in person. I would do anything for you, Dara. But I don't know what it is you think I can do. I'm just a fire elemental witch."

She held out her hand, a small ball of flame erupting in her palm.

I shook my head as Sawyer handed me bread and a bowl of soup.

"Eat."

He looked at Cruz. "I would ask if you would want to eat too, but I don't know the protocol of feeding a wolf."

Cruz lifted a brow. "Protocol?"

"I've only met a few shifters in passing. So I don't know if I'm allowed to feed such a dominant wolf or if you must feed yourself. If you're supposed to eat first or how that goes."

Cruz looked at Sawyer, blinked, and burst out laughing. A subtle and low laugh that seemed to pull me out of whatever funk I'd been falling into. "It's not like the movies. I'm just a man here. I'm happy with whatever you fed her. French onion? It smells divine."

Sawyer grinned. "I was in the mood to cook. And Jade had a feeling that we would need the warmth."

I stared down at the soup, and then up at Cruz, before I looked back to Jade. "Things are changing. I'm worried. I know you have never wanted to be part of the Pack business. But we need you. Please."

Jade nodded and sighed. "There's a reason I've never wanted to be in the Pack. And he's standing in this room."

I froze, confused, as Cruz looked between us.

"What?" he asked, his voice low. "I've never met you before, Jade. Why would I be the reason?"

"Your mother, of course. Don't you know?"

The magic around us dimmed and Sawyer straightened. Cruz did too, as I froze, afraid of what Jade would reveal.

And what it would break.

CHAPTER NINE

Cruz

I stiffened, staring at the fire witch. The magic in the room pushed at my wolf, giving me a headache.

I didn't mind magic, it helped keep our Pack safe, and my mate was a fucking witch after all. I called her that even though the bond would never come and she would never be mine, but I still felt the pull. The mating urge would never go away. I still wanted to feel her under me, to feel that bond snap into place and show her that there was a reason fate had destined us.

But the rest of me knew that would never happen.

I trusted magic in the same ways that I trusted shifters. Somewhat, and only with cause.

I did not trust this witch in front of me and the way that she glared at me, yet she had a curiosity in that gaze that worried me at the same time.

"I have never met you. You say you've never wanted to be part of our Pack, fine. But I don't know you. What do you have against me? And how the hell did you know my mother?"

My wolf pushed at me, wanting out. The shift wasn't easy, it hurt, it took every ounce of your control not to scream in agony as bones broke and tendons tore and you became the wolf or bear or cat within you.

I shared a body with another soul, the two of us becoming one as we blended into the power that we had as animal and human. But right then and there, my wolf wanted to be in control, and I was afraid I wanted to let it. Because I wasn't sure I wanted to know the answers that this woman would give.

"I knew your mother. I know who you are, Cruz."

"What are you talking about, Jade?" Dara stood up a little shakily, and I glared at her.

"Sit back down," I said at the same time as her friend. I glared at Jade, before turning back to Dara. "You need to rest. Stop it."

"No, I will not stop it. I want to know what's going on. How do you know his mother, Jade? And why have you never spoken to me about it?"

"Because I didn't know that you knew him. I'm sorry. I honest to God thought you knew about your mother."

"You're going to want to explain very quickly, in clear words. Because I don't appreciate you speaking about my mother as if you knew her." That familiar pain that came when thinking about my mother hit me, but I let it go, telling myself to breathe.

"I knew your mother, because she kept me safe long ago, when she was still hiding from your father. The man who threatened her. Who threatened all of us."

I was in front of Jade in an instant, towering over her as I glared. Sawyer moved quickly, but he was still human, and I snarled at him as he held up his hands and I noticed the blade in each.

"You're going to want to step away from Jade. Don't threaten my friend."

"She's speaking of things she doesn't understand."

"No, I really think it's you that doesn't understand," Jade said as she stared up at me. She didn't look worried, she looked confused.

"How did you know my mother?"

"Because she saved my life. And when she was tired one night, she told me why she was on the run. I was just a kid, a kid like you. You and I never met, but I was there when they found her. When they told us that you would forever be Pack. She was so worried about you. You don't remember any of this?"

"What the hell are you talking about?"

Dara stood at my side. I wanted to growl at her, to tell her to sit back down, but there was no stopping her, not just then. "Jade. You're not making any sense. How could you know his mother? She died before I became Pack."

"I know that," Jade snapped. "She died right before *he* came."

Bile slid up my throat as my entire body turned to ice, and the whispers of why I had become Heir slid through me. Why I held the position I did in the Pack when I shouldn't.

"Who do you mean *he*?" I asked, afraid I knew the answer.

"Blade. The man who took her will and gave her a son. The Alpha of the Aspen Pack. Your father."

I shook my head, scrambling back, even as my wolf snarled and fought. "What the hell are you talking about? Blade was not my father. That monster can't be."

"He was. He took you away from her when you were just a kid. Long before any of us were born."

Considering I was eighty years old, it made sense. The timing checked out. But I didn't want to think like that. I couldn't if I wanted to breathe.

"How? What? This doesn't make any sense. Blade can't be his father. His mother and Blade weren't mates. And shifters can only have children with those they mate with."

A pained expression cross Jade's face, and she shook her head. "Not unless you use dark magics." I didn't even realize I was moving forward until Jade held up her hand, flames tickling around her fingertips. "I know you're angry, but you need to control your wolf. You're stronger than this. You're strong, like your mother."

"Don't talk about my mother. I am not that abomination's son." But what if it was true? No, it couldn't be true.

"You're telling me that the former Alpha of the Aspen Pack, Chase's father, is also Cruz's father?" Dara asked, her words hitting me like a brick to the face.

Chase. My Alpha. My friend.

No, he couldn't be my brother. That wasn't how this works.

"My mother said my father died long ago. Before I was even born. She was pregnant with me, when her mate died. That was the only way it all made sense."

"Did she say that? To protect you? Because I thought you knew. I wouldn't have brought this all up otherwise. Not while we're trying to deal with the coven and find the magics to protect our people. I'm sorry, I thought you knew."

"I don't fucking know." My head began to pulse and my wolf whined. Something was wrong. So fucking wrong. And not just with what they were saying. No...it was as if something was inside me other than my wolf, and it was trying to get out. It tasted of old magic and I needed to say it. To tell the others. But I couldn't fucking breathe.

"Everyone just calm down," Sawyer said as he slid his blades back into the boots I hadn't known he wore. Why hadn't I noticed? I narrowed my gaze at him and realized that Jade must have used some magic to hide them. I would have to think about that later.

"My mother died before the war with the Talon Pack. When Blade was still Alpha and using dark magic. I grew up in the Aspens because she wanted me to have a home. But she never joined for her own reasons."

Reasons that never made any sense to me, but I hadn't voiced it then. Because she was my mother.

Dara turned to me then, frowning. "She didn't become Pack, but she let *you*?"

I frowned, thinking back. "She said that she hadn't wanted to be part of her old Pack, that she wanted the freedom. I just assumed that's how it worked for her. There are lone wolves out there."

"Yet she let her son become Pack?"

"She was always welcome in the den."

"But did she go?"

I ran my hand over my face, trying to think. It was as if a haze slid over me, and everything that I thought was real was not.

"Damn it. Why didn't I figure this out sooner? There's a spell on him, trying to mess up his memories. There's something wrong," Jade said and moved towards me.

"My goddess. How did we miss that? How did all of us miss that?" Dara cursed. "Cruz, I didn't see it before because it's so old, but can I lift it? The spell on your memories."

I whirled. "What fucking magic is on me?" I asked, my voice ice.

Jade cursed under her breath, but Dara stood there, eyes defiant, and held out her hand.

"I don't know. It's not my magic, and it's not Jade's. If I had to bet, it's probably from the dark witch that Blade used to taint the Pack all those years ago. He always liked secrets, it was the reason that many of our friends were hidden, and how we were hidden for so long. It would make sense that he had more secrets. Hell, I was a secret to most of the den and I lived with you guys."

I shook my head. "Take away the spell. I want to remember." Even though I really didn't. The magic deep inside pulsed and my wolf ached, scared when I couldn't be. My wolf was *never* scared.

Dara held out her hand and Jade took it without being asked. They each put a hand on my temples, and I fell to my knees, pain slicing through me like a hot poker. I screamed, and Dara and Jade said something, which I assumed was to Sawyer, as I shook and tried not to throw up.

"What the hell was that?" I asked. But then I had my own answers.

Because the reason that nothing made sense about my past was because it really *wasn't* my past. Everything unspooled.

"Dear goddess," I whispered.

Dara knelt in front of me, cupping my face. "It's okay. Tell us what you see. What you remember."

"Mom. She was Pack. She was Aspen. But that doesn't make any sense. She told me she was a lone wolf, that's why she never stayed in the den."

All those conversations with her, us hiding. I thought it had been to hide from her old Pack, which ended up being true. She had been hiding from Blade. I shook my head and stood up, taking Dara with me. Jade and Sawyer were setting out tea, Jade muttering under her breath.

"I'm going to give you something for the nausea, and the headache that's bound to come. I am sorry. Truly. I see that whatever dark witch Blade used liked the forceful spells. I didn't sense it on you until we were talking, and that was probably just one part of the spell."

Dara continued. "Meaning, they wanted to hide who you were all this time. I bet with that spell broken, the rest of the den will soon start to remember your mother, Cruz. Exactly who she was. As soon as you enter the wards, the spell that we've broken here will break across the rest of the den."

I shook my head, trying to keep up, and failing. "My mother and Blade weren't mates. That changes the rules of mating." I looked at Dara, eyes wide. "Blade is my father. I remember it now. The screaming, him pulling me back into the den. Mom tried to hide, but he forced me to live within the den for as long as I did. He wanted to control me, to have a fucking spare," I spat.

"And your mother tried to protect you," Jade said. "I'm sorry. I'm sorry for putting it all out there like this."

It felt as if someone had dipped me into something putrid. "The man who fathered me was a monster. A fucking monster who killed so many." I swallowed hard. "Who killed my mother."

"I'm sorry, Cruz."

I shook my head. "I guess it makes sense why I'm the Heir now. No one could understand how I ended up in the position, second in command, because it's usually by bloodline. But we all assumed because Chase didn't have any blood relations left, that it went to someone random within the den. But apparently I was always the blood relation. The spawn of Blade. His bastard."

I paced, and Dara moved forward. "It doesn't change who you are."

I whirled.

"It changes everything. That fucking man ruined our Pack. Broke us. Killed and hurt so many of us. And his blood runs in my veins. I was his dirty secret, and I never knew."

"And none of it changes who you are."

"I'm not so sure about that."

I whirled, leaving the room, needing to breathe. I didn't bother to see if they followed me. We had scores to settle, magic to burn, and people to save. But right then, I could only think about one thing.

Blade was my father.

I was the son of a monster.

It was no wonder that the bonds of fate, the goddess, and future wouldn't form.

I was never meant to exist at all.

CHAPTER TEN

Dara

"I NEED TO GO AFTER HIM."

I turned to Jade, who nodded solemnly. "Be careful."

"Of course, I will be. We have wards and will be on the lookout."

"Then yes, go. I'll pack up what I need to, and then we can go with you."

I turned to Jade's friend, the human man I didn't know very well, but knew would do anything to protect his friend. "This isn't your fight. You don't have to do this."

He just snorted and looked over at Jade. "Yes, I do. Jade is my family. And that means you are too. And if you think the vampires are going to stop with the witches and the Packs, you don't really understand your enemy that well, do you? Where do you think they are getting all these vampires?"

I winced, then looked through the open door where Cruz had walked off.

"Go. We'll be fine here. You just make sure he's okay. I didn't realize that he hadn't known. I wouldn't have blurted it all out like that."

I turned to one of my best friends, or at least the woman that I had known for the longest, and scowled.

"Why didn't you ever tell me?"

"Because at first it wasn't my business, and how was I supposed to know you two were mates?"

I shook my head. "No. We're not mates."

The pain in my voice was loud enough that it sounded as if it were a scream in my ears.

Jade held up her hands, eyes wide. "Okay, it seems we have a lot to discuss. Because I see the two of you."

"We can't mate, and you know damn well why we can't. You can sense it between us. But I need to follow him, to make sure he's okay. He came out on this journey with me, to find witches for us, and yet he's the one being hurt by it. He came here to protect me, and all I've done is get him hurt, in every way possible."

"I don't believe any of that's on you," Sawyer said with a frown.

"I'm not so sure about that."

Before they could say anything else, I left them to

pack, to get ready to begin our next phase as a coven, as a collection of witches with powers from more than just elementals. I needed to see Cruz, even though I knew it would only hurt us both in the end.

I didn't know what I should say, what I could say, but I needed to do something.

I turned the corner and Cruz stood there, not outside in the alley, but right near the door, hands braced against the doorway, chest heaving.

"Cruz?" I asked, and he didn't turn, though his body stiffened.

I knew he heard me come closer, had scented me long before I had spoken. Because this was Cruz, the Heir of the Aspen Pack. He was such a dominant wolf, his connection to that wolf strong enough that it dwarfed others. No matter what he was feeling, no matter the horror that he might deal with deep inside, he was still Cruz. Always in control, ready to protect. I wouldn't catch him unawares.

"I know you must be in pain, and I don't know what I'm supposed to say. I want to make things easier for you, but I don't think there is a way to do that. So I'll just say I'm sorry."

He turned slowly, his eyes narrowed and gold. I was looking at the wolf now, not just the man.

I always loved looking at Cruz—the way that he stood straight, forceful in any situation. He might yell at me more often than not, might not know what to do with me, but this was Cruz, the man I had fallen for before I meant to.

His dark hair looked as if he had run his hands through it a few times, and his beard was coming in nicely, as he hadn't shaved since we'd been on the road. He was tall, his shoulders broad, all muscle.

I had wanted him from the first time I saw him, even though I hadn't realized why until it was almost too late.

"If you keep staring at me like that, I'm going to press you against that wall and show you exactly how dominant I am. It doesn't matter that both of us know it would be a mistake."

I steeled myself at that, a little out of breath. "We should talk. Before we head to one of our final destinations. We should talk."

"Two more witches, is that what you said? And you can't just call them up so I can keep you safe behind the wards before someone else finds us?"

"They won't answer. They've been in hiding for longer than I ever was. They won't come to us unless I plead my case in person. And with what we want from them, it's a show of respect."

"Maybe. Or maybe it feels like we're running from power to power, as someone hunts us. But then again, you've had the hunter next to you this whole time."

I shook my head as I moved close to him, and I hadn't even realized my hand was on his chest until we both stiffened, and I could feel his heartbeat beneath my palm.

"We can talk. About anything you want. Or we can leave right now and go find the final two witches, and then try to work their power to keep our people safe. Because that's what you do, Cruz, you keep us safe."

He snorted. "Is this what you call safe? There are people coming after you. What else did you want to talk about? About the fact that my father was a monster? Or that I can't have my mate because death surrounds us? How about that."

I flinched, I couldn't help it, and I knew it was the wrong thing to do as he glared.

"Blade was a monster. And he might have donated the genes that made you, but you are nothing like him. And how can you even think that? Especially because you know Chase. Our Alpha was raised by that man, and yet he is so much stronger than any of us. He's our Alpha, and I trust him with my life, and that's not something I ever thought I would say."

"I find it odd that Jade knew my mother, and sometimes it feels like I didn't."

"I don't know why I didn't know."

He tilted his head, studied my face. "Would you have told me? If you had known my mother."

I thought for a second, and as he scowled, I nodded.

"I would have. I would've found another way to tell you. Because despite the fact that our relationship—if you can call it that—is so complicated I don't even have a title for it, we've always been friends. We fought side by side, and I've watched you lead quietly, beside Chase. You are the Heir for a reason."

"Genetics."

"No. I believed you were the Heir because of what you brought. Not because of who Blade was."

He paced, and I let him, not sure what to say. He was always the one taking care of me, when I was too weak to stand, when the magic from keeping the wards in place nearly killed me, he was the one to stand by my side, to keep me afloat. What else was I supposed to do? What was I supposed to say?

"My mother was stronger than anyone I knew, even Chase. And the more I think about it, the more I think about who she was at that time, I realize that I didn't really know her."

"When we get back to the den, I can look more now that I understand that it was there. That spell? I can try to make sure that nothing's there at all so that way you can untangle those memories. To make it make sense."

He snorted, but there was no humor in it.

"I don't think it will ever make sense. Not the way that we both need it to. My mother was always so scared. But I hadn't realized it was because of him." He let out a breath. "My father hurt my mother. I can see that now. He killed her, and he took me away from her. But she spent her entire life trying to protect me. And I wasn't strong enough to help her."

"You were a child."

"I was a dominant wolf."

"And she wouldn't want you to carry that pain. I might not have known her, but I see her in the way that you care for others. Know that you are not your father's son."

He opened his mouth to say something but I continued before he could. "My parents were strong, but not as strong as me. They didn't have my magic, but they tried to protect me. And the other coven killed them for it. I can still hear their screams, and I can hear them trying to save me, and I couldn't save them. I lived on the street after that, with these people that you're meeting now. And we became our own family until it was too dangerous for us to be together."

"Until Blade tricked you into coming to the Aspens where he tried to force your magic into something it wasn't."

"And that was on him, never on you. You never did that. None of the Aspens have tried to corrupt my death magic."

"We've never wanted you to hurt your soul for it."

"And that is the strength of your wolf."

"I need time to breathe. I just need to think."

He turned and left me, walking down the alley, still within Jade's inner wards, but he left me.

"I can still sense him. He's not going off far. Let him breathe. And then you have to go meet the others."

"Bishop and Leta. They're the last two. And I can't get ahold of them any other way than seeing them face to face.

But we've been gone from the den for too long. It feels like longer, but it's only been a couple of days. But it's still too long."

"Well, send us to the den. We'll do our best to protect them. Though I would rather be with you. Stand by your side."

"I bring death wherever I go," I said, though I hadn't meant to.

"You're a death witch. But what's the other side of death? Life. Remember that. You aren't some soul eater."

"That's not what the other witches say," I mumbled.

"Then they don't know you very well, do they? We're almost done packing and then we'll leave. We'll meet with Declan, then go to the den and see what we can do about the wards. You've warned the others that we're coming, right? And that we all need to be on the lookout for whatever is coming?"

I nodded. "Yes. They're not going to let anyone in that they haven't vetted yet, but they know that you're coming to help."

"It'll be weird, working with the wolves, working with someone who doesn't think that we're inherently evil because we're not perfect happy little earth witches."

My lips twitched. "One of the strongest witches I know is an earth witch, a Healer, and she could drown a man in the earth itself if he comes after her pups."

"Hannah. I've heard of this witch. The Redwood

Princess who could take over the world with her kind smile. I'd like to meet her."

"You will. We should have done this long ago. Protected all of us."

"We couldn't. We weren't ready yet. Now go find your man."

"He's not my man."

"Then we'll fix that. Because you deserve happiness, Dara. Of all of us, you deserve happiness."

And with that she walked off, leaving me alone in the doorway, shaking my head.

We needed to find Bishop and then Leta, the final two witches that I knew would create this coven. Without the collection of powers, we wouldn't be able to stop the vampires. There was no other way. We needed to stop this. So we would.

Even if it felt like we were running in circles, chasing our tails while the monsters followed us, stronger and faster and with a stronger bite.

I stepped into the alley, needing the air, knowing that we needed to leave soon. I could sense Cruz near, pacing, because my own powers reached out to him without even thinking. Wanting to wrap around him and keep him close.

I just wasn't sure why I couldn't hold on.

There had to be a way to break the tattered bond between us. I had brought him back from death, and in doing so I had irrevocably altered who we were. There had to be a way to change that, and maybe with the coven of new powers, we'd be able to. Because each time I used my magic, each time I tried to protect my den, I pulled on both of us, on the essence of who we were.

I was dying. I knew it.

But I was so afraid that as I took that last breath, I would bring Cruz with me, and that was something I refused.

Heat brushed my side and I turned as light slammed into me. I fell off the steps, my knee scraping against the stonework, as bright magic slammed into me once, twice.

It tasted familiar, something I should know, and yet it wasn't right. There was something corrupted about it.

I stood up and slammed my hands up into the air, bringing forth the harvester magic.

My magic wasn't elemental. As I pulled into myself, I wasn't using souls per se, but death itself. The absence of life. As life surrounded us, so did death. So I used both to create a kinetic energy and pushed it towards my attacker.

"Who are you?" I screamed, but I couldn't hear over the din of wind and power. Magic pushed at me again, and I slammed through the brick wall to the side, out of Jade's wards and out of hearing range of the others.

Whatever picked me up and tossed me into the air, pushed me into the street two alleys over, and I scrambled up, moving that kinetic energy back towards my attacker. I couldn't see them, because it was as if they were using the light itself to reflect back at me, blinding me. Someone was in front of me, fighting me, but I didn't know who it was, and they were using powers that I didn't think were their own.

Just like I used death and life that weren't mine, they were using something else. But it wasn't light, no, it was the absence of it. Darkness itself.

And as they slammed into me again, the magic cutting into me, I shot out my hand, pushing the harvester power forward. It clutched at the person in front of me, and while I wanted to pull back, wrench their soul from their body and shout to the heavens, I knew that wasn't what I should do. But I needed to stop them, to push them back.

They screamed, and once again I noted that this person was familiar. I knew them, they were the one following us, the one who killed Iris, but who were they?

And then the light slammed into me again, cutting into my chest and my face and my leg, and I hit the ground. My head aching, I was unable to stand.

Footsteps sounded as my attacker left, but I didn't know why, didn't know what had scared them away.

Everything hurt, as blood pooled around me, I knew I wasn't strong enough.

The wards within me pulsed, and I was so afraid that if I didn't stand up, didn't fight back again, the wards of the den, even miles and miles away, would fall. I was the one keeping them aloft, keeping my den safe. I needed to stay awake.

But there was nothing.

Only a whispered word, the prophecy that I ignored. The one that I hadn't wanted to think of.

Death is righting a wrong for a past forsaken. The lost son will return, and the tears of pain and agony will dry. Though the sacrifice of cost of an action will never be equal, but will return threefold.

Death would come. But it would right a wrong.

Someone would return, but would I leave?

I couldn't think, couldn't tear down that prophecy. Instead I lay my head on the cold asphalt, and tried to reach out.

"Cruz," I whispered, though no words came out. Just a raspy breath.

Cruz would find me. I knew he would.

Because if he didn't, if I died here, so would he.

I refused to let it, but as the darkness came, I didn't know what hope I had left.

CHAPTER ELEVEN

Cruz

My wolf threatened to peek out, the stress more than either of us wanted. I let out a breath, and let my claws slide from beneath my fingertips. Shifting into a wolf wasn't easy. Most shifts took blood, sweat, tears, and pain in order to go from one form to another. I could sense every single pinprick of sensation as my claws slid out of my fingertips, as my fangs elongated. But it was a welcome pain, one that quickly turned into bliss that told me that I was doing this for a reason. That I was my own power.

The shifters were out in the world now, there was no reason to hide this other than for good PR, and not to scare some poor unsuspecting human as they walked past. But I was at the edge of Jade's wards, and we were as safe as we could be within them. Although I wasn't sure how well they could last against an onslaught of the magic we had been seeing. I wasn't even sure if Jade had seen this magic before. For all I knew, the monsters that hunted us all were just waiting for the right moment. I kept thinking about all of that, because if I didn't, I would have to deal with the idea that a monster's blood ran through my veins.

Everything made sense now, the way that Blade had either ignored or paid too much attention to me.

Blade had wanted to rule over the Talon Pack, and the other Packs in the US. And in order to do that, he had aligned with a dark witch and claimed her as his butchered mate, even though they hadn't had the proper bond.

He started a great war between factions, one that I had fought in, but not on the side he wanted.

I had been strong enough to break the call of the Alpha. To push back against his order for me to kill the Talon Pack, like many of us had. And the ones who hadn't been strong enough to defy the Alpha, we had hidden. They had cried in pain and curled into balls, mostly in wolf form, as they had tried to go against their Alpha's wishes.

All of us had done what we could to protect the others. It hadn't always been easy, but we had tried.

I had been able to do it because of my dominance, because he was my father. Just like Chase had eventually been able to break through the bindings that had captured him for so long.

Audrey had been the first to defy him, stronger than all of us combined.

The Beta of the Aspen Pack had always been the most courageous, the most forceful, all to protect her people when no one else could.

When Blade died, a new hierarchy had entered into the Aspen Pack.

Audrey had stayed as Beta, and the rest of us had changed. I was no longer a soldier, fighting for a war I didn't believe in, but now I was the Heir, Chase's left hand. And now his brother.

"Holy hell."

"That doesn't sound good," a very familiar voice said. I whirled, ready to swipe out, when I froze at a familiar face.

Steele, my best friend and training partner, stood there, brows raised. "Are you just going to tear out my throat without even thinking? Not very nice, Heir."

"What the hell are you doing here?" I asked, looking around. "And why didn't I scent you?"

"I'm using one of Dara's little herb packets to hide my scent. The one that she's testing? Seems it's working. Between that and being downwind, it's good. Though your wolf is all up in arms right now, so not quite sure why he didn't see me."

I ran my hands over my face, grateful my claws and

fangs were gone. I was back to being human, but fucking lost.

"What's wrong, brother?" Steele asked, and I stiffened.

I hadn't meant to, because Steele always saw far too much for my own good, but he just stared at me.

"Are you going to tell me what's going on? Where's your witch. Is she okay?" he asked.

I shook my head. "She's fine," I said, because I knew the shake of my head had probably confused him. "She's with the other witch. And a human."

"Honestly, that raises more questions than answering any of them. I'm the Enforcer, Cruz. It's my job to protect the Pack from outside forces. You telling us you are sending us all these witches with such immense power and that we're supposed to trust them even though I don't know them isn't really helping my wolf right now."

I let out a hollow laugh, understanding what Steele meant far too well. "I think it's the only way."

"Well, that's not mysterious at all. What the hell's going on, Cruz? Dara's having prophecy visions in front of us at the den house, and now the two of you are suddenly acting as if you guys have a long history when I didn't even realize you two were friends. What haven't you told us?"

I looked around, realized where we were standing nobody else could really see or hear us, but I was still worried.

"I came alone. My lieutenants and soldiers are

protecting the den. Being at a heightened state of panic and war isn't good for any of us. We're safe for now."

"You can't come any closer though, Jade's wards won't let you."

Steele sniffed. "I sensed them. That's why I haven't moved forward to beat your ass for just standing there and not telling me what the hell's going on. This Jade seems strong, though, she'd be good for the Pack."

"I don't think she necessarily wants to become Pack, maybe coven."

Steele sneered. "Yes, because the coven's done so much for us all."

"They used to. Then something happened. We should fix that."

"It looks to me like you are."

"There's something I need to tell you."

"About your witch?"

I froze, then realized maybe he should hear the whole story. Maybe I should tell him what I had been hiding from everybody for far too long. I'd have to tell my Alpha. It was past time. But how did I tell him he was my brother?

I swallowed hard, my bile rising far too quickly.

"On the battlefield, that day against Valac and Sunny. Do you remember?"

"Are you talking about the time that Dara fell to her knees to save your ass? You were hit pretty hard, man. We all felt it."

I shook my head, the scent of smoke and fire filling my nostrils, as if I were right back there on the battlefield. "She didn't just save me, Cruz. She brought me back."

Steele frowned. "What the hell are you talking about?"

"I died. Right then and there. I died, and Dara brought me back."

"You mean you were hurt, and she healed you."

I shook my head, my wolf pacing. "No. I *died.* Dara brought me back. Because she's my mate, and was able to use whatever bond we could have had, and the fact that she's a harvester death witch. She brought me back. I don't know exactly how it worked, but it did, and ever since then, we've been connected, but not in the way that we should. Not in the way that true mates are. I'm fucking draining her power. Every time she uses her magic, every time she tries to protect the wards and fight against the vampires because she's the only strong witch we have, she dies a little. Because of me. We can never complete the mating bond because there's already one there, one that's wrong and jagged and it's my fault."

I hadn't meant to say all that, I had meant to talk about Blade, but apparently I couldn't hold onto any more secrets. And this was Steele, he deserved to know. Or maybe I just needed to get the words out.

Steele looked at me then, eyes wide, looking as if he were trying to say something, only his mouth just opened and closed like a blowfish. I actually had never seen him at a loss for words before, it was quite refreshing. Even as I felt I was going to be sick.

"Everything makes a lot more fucking sense right now, but goddess. Are you serious? Is there anything we can do? For Dara? She's your mate. And she's a damn good mate for you. The person I would have chosen."

"What?" I asked, blinking. "You would've chosen Dara."

"Wouldn't you? You guys butt heads against each other more often than not. You guys balance each other's strengths. You're quiet until you're not, and she's always a force. She needs someone steady. Someone who knows what the fuck he's doing because she is the center of our core strength right now. She's just as dominant as you. Maybe a little more," he said with a laugh. Then he sobered. "We need to fix this. Maybe these witches that you're bringing together can." Steele looked up at the wards that he couldn't actually see, but we could both feel. "Maybe this Jade can help her. Or that asshole Declan."

I narrowed my gaze. "You've met him?"

"Yes. He reminds me of Spike from *Buffy the Vampire Slayer* for some reason. I have no idea why, but he does."

"We're trying to fight against the vampires, not bring them in," I said, trying to find humor in the situation.

"Well, he did sacrifice himself in the end. Spoilers?" Steele asked, and I knew he was trying to alleviate the tension, even if it didn't make any sense.

"There's something else that you're not telling me, but

that was a lot, and I'm glad that you finally said something. Now, are you going to let me in? Or am I going to stand out here until you can show me your witch, and this new one. And you said something about a human? Her mate?"

I shook my head, about to say something and get Jade, when the earth rumbled beneath my feet. Something within my heart twisted, as if that tattered bond I hadn't even realized was there until recently snapped closed. It pulsed once, twice, before it sizzled, and I leaned back, my eyes wide.

"Dara's in trouble."

I whirled, my feet slapping against the concrete as I moved, and I heard Steele curse.

"This is going to fucking hurt," Steele muttered, before he slammed into the wards, his skin sizzling just enough to have smoke waft off his body, before he crushed through them and kept moving.

I was fast, but Steele was faster, and soon we were both running past Jade's place, her and Sawyer tumbling out of the house.

"How the hell did you break through my wards?" Jade asked.

"I don't know, I'm just special. What the hell was that?" Steele asked, the two of them glaring at each other.

"I don't feel the same magic you do, but since there's a hole in the wall over there, I'm going to go that way," Sawyer said as he pointed towards the hole in the brick wall with his knife.

I whirled, scenting Dara, moving before I could even think. I jumped through the hole, past the people shouting at one another, and kept moving down one street, then the other.

Dara was hurt and I didn't know how bad. I hadn't even known she'd been taken. I was too busy feeling sorry for myself and growling at Steele, and I hadn't been there.

"Seriously, how did you do that?"

"I don't know, but they packed a punch. I think they're fine, but dammit, next time just let me in."

"I didn't even realize you wanted through, or the fact that you wanted to see your friend. Next time call ahead," Jade growled at Steele.

I knew they were snapping at each other because they were afraid for Dara, but it didn't matter. Because I could scent Dara's blood, and everything within me screamed.

Dara lay on the ground, blood pooling around her, her hair billowing around her face. Her hand was flung out, as if reaching out towards something, but she laid there, unmoving, in a crumpled heap.

I knelt at her side, grateful I could see her chest rising and falling, even shallowly.

"You, check that corner," Steele ordered Sawyer. Sawyer glared, but did as he was told.

Everybody knew who Steele was, it was hard to escape the Enforcer of the Aspen Pack in the media, even if Steele tried to hide from it. Given that, and his dominance, everyone listened to what he said. Steele searched around for whoever had done this. I wanted to join, but first I needed to make sure Dara was okay.

"Let me see her," Jade ordered, as she pushed away my hand. I growled at her, snapping my fangs, and she just waved me off.

"I might be a fire witch, but I can also heal. Her spine's intact, so we can move her to my place where all my things are. And then we can move her to your next witch."

"What the hell happened?" I asked, my voice so icy cold I knew it could snuff out her fire in an instant.

She looked at me, the anger in her gaze outmatched by the pain. This was her friend, and she was hurting just like I was.

I didn't know how I was supposed to handle this. Because Dara was mine, even though she couldn't be.

And if I hadn't left her, hadn't wanted to brood, she wouldn't be hurt.

"Stop fucking blaming yourself, wolf, and pick up your mate and take her to my house. I don't scent any other magic users here, and it was magic that did this. Magic I haven't seen before. If this is what we're going up against, I'm glad we're building a new coven. A full one. Because this magic is an abomination, and we need to pull it out. Dara's going to be fine, I won't let anything else happen. I want to know who the hell did this, and you, wolf, I know you're right along with me."

I met Jade's gaze, and I knew right then and there we

were on the same page, and we would do anything for Dara.

I didn't tell the other woman that Dara wasn't my mate. I couldn't.

Because even without a bond, I knew I would never let her go.

Even without a bond, I knew she was mine.

But I needed to keep her safe first.

And find out who the hell did this and rip out their spine.

CHAPTER

TWELVE

Dara

"I'm fine. Stop hovering." I sighed, running my hands over my hair. I still had a headache, there was no stopping that thanks to the magics used, but I wasn't bleeding anymore, and Jade had fixed me up to the best of her abilities. Neither of us were true healers like some witches, but we knew enough to get by. I would be forever grateful that Jade had been there when I was found, because I honestly wasn't sure how much longer I would've lasted lying on the ground in my own blood. But I didn't want to say that to Cruz, not when he was scowling at me, eyes narrowed, the gold glowing enough to radiate over the hardwood floors.

"You're not fine. You almost died."

"We're at war with magical creatures. We all almost

die far too often for my own liking. But I'm fine. I promise you. We can go soon."

"We're staying the night," he snapped, his wolf rising once again.

I met Jade's gaze, who just raised an imperious brow, and went back to making a plate of food.

"We don't need to sit here and wait for me to heal any more than I already have. Jade did her work, and now we have to go."

"And you know that Leta and Bishop won't see you yet. It's too late in the day."

I cringed. "Because healing my weak self took too long."

"You aren't weak," Cruz snapped, getting right in my face. I could feel the heat of him, the worry, and I knew he was scared. Hell, I had been scared too. But I couldn't think about it too hard. Because I was afraid of what could have happened, and if I focused on it for too long, I would just make things worse. I knew how this worked. How it all worked.

"We don't have time for me to sit around and wallow. We need to go and meet with the others. We don't have time. Clearly we don't have time."

"Tell me exactly what happened again, and then I'll think about it," Cruz ordered.

And it was an order. It couldn't be anything else.

Behind him, Steele rolled his eyes, but I still saw the order in his gaze as well. I hadn't been awake when the

Enforcer had shown up, but I was glad he was here. I didn't know exactly what secrets Cruz had told him. What secrets were now out in the world. I would ask, but not in front of the others.

But with the way that Steele watched me, he knew something, and I needed to know what. But I was glad he was here for Cruz no matter what.

I had a feeling that Cruz would need him more often than not in the coming days.

"Why were you out there alone?" Steele asked, and this time it was Cruz who flinched.

"I was out there alone beneath the first set of wards just to breathe. To formulate the next plan to get Bishop and Leta. Because once we have them, we can complete the coven and finally have a chance against the vampires. I am allowed to walk alone, especially beneath wards."

"And yet you got hurt."

"Some magic pulled at me, something crushed that side of the wards, a power I've never tasted before."

"It tasted of light," Jade put in, frowning. "But it was wrong somehow. As if it's been twisted. Or perhaps a culmination of things?"

I met the other witch's solemn gaze.

And she paled.

"I think it's the person who took Henrick's power. The same person that took Iris's. They're using it somehow. They aren't just siphoning off the magic, but they're using it to create this abomination."

"Does this mean they're stronger than what we can pull together?"

I shook my head, ignoring the headache that was finally dissipating. "I'm not saying that. We are stronger together than we are apart—Pack, human, witch. All of us. We can be stronger than this person, whoever they are. But I don't know who they were. It was just different."

"And they attacked you out of the blue?"

"I didn't provoke them other than existing. Something you sure damn well know."

"I wasn't blaming you. I just wanted to get the lay of the land. You were hurt. Pardon me for my wolf being out of its fucking mind."

My heart did that funny lurching thing as I met his gaze, and the three other people in the room seemed to disappear, as if they didn't matter. Though they did, and yet all I wanted was to kiss him, to tell him it was okay. To lean into the fact that our bond could be there if fate hadn't gotten in the way. But it wasn't going to happen and I needed to remember that.

"I'm fine," I whispered, as I put my hand over his chest, his heartbeat racing but steady. I hated this, the unknowing, but we weren't the center of this. We weren't what was important. Not in this moment, not when so many people relied on us.

"What else happened?" Steele asked, cutting through the tension. And though I was grateful for his interruption, I still resented it.

"Whatever light magic, or dark mist, or whatever they used sliced through me, and I hit my head when I went down. They didn't siphon magic from me." I closed my eyes and held onto my own magic. "That much I know, and I don't know why they didn't. Maybe you guys coming for me stopped them, or maybe they had another agenda, I don't know. But they didn't, and while that worries me, I had the prophecy whispered in my mind again."

Both Jade and Sawyer looked at me with a frown, Jade's eyes intent. Steele and Cruz cursed.

"What does that mean? What the hell does the prophecy have to do with this?"

"I'm not sure, but I think I know who needs to come home. My way."

I met Cruz's gaze and his eyes widened for a moment, before he cursed and moved away to pace.

"What is she talking about?" Sawyer asked.

"I don't know, but she's going to tell me soon. If you do what I think you're wanting to do, even if I don't know who, you already know what happened once. It could break you."

Steele growled, and I shook my head.

"I don't think it will be like before. I don't think it can be." Because I was already broken, they couldn't shatter me again, not in that way. And I already had that tattered bond with Cruz. I couldn't have another. But perhaps I could do what was needed because my magic was evolving. And because the prophecy was leading towards it.

Or maybe I was just thinking too hard about things that couldn't be.

"Enough of this," Cruz ordered, and everyone glared at him. "She needs rest, and we need to get the two of you out of here." He pointed towards Sawyer and Jade. "You need to get back to the den, all of you."

Steele raised a brow. "I'm not leaving you alone."

"You need to warn the Pack and get things ready. Because things are still happening here. You know what to do. And we need to finish our tasks."

"What's been happening at the Pack?" I asked, needing to get the attention off my own issues and onto everyone else. Steele looked between us, his jaw tightening.

"We've had a few more scuffles with the vampires, and we still don't know who their general is, or who's leading them."

"Somebody has to be orchestrating this," I said quickly.

"The other one was Valac?" Jade asked, tapping her fingers against the wood of the hutch next to her.

"And how do you know that?" Steele asked, accusation in his tone.

"I know that because I watch the news. You might think you're the center of the universe within your wards and dealing with your own wars, but the world is watching. We all are."

"I don't think we need to snap at each other when

we're all on the same side," Sawyer began, placating, but Steele just turned his sharp gaze towards the human.

"I don't know who you are, or what you're doing here. But I don't need you trying to mediate between us."

Sawyer just raised a brow. "One of us has to because it's not going to be the two dominant wolves in this room, nor is it going to be the witches with enough power in their pinkie to probably raze this entire area."

My lips twitched even though there was nothing funny about this situation. Sawyer seemed to be good at mediating, and I wondered how he and Jade were such close friends, and why he was willing to risk everything for her. But it wasn't my place to ask, at least not in front of everybody else.

"What else? About the Pack. And stop fighting with each other. We already said we're on the same side, at least for this. So drop it."

Steele glared at Sawyer, before he shrugged as if he had no cares in the world. I knew that was a lie, as the Enforcer cared too much—that was his problem. "We're training, fighting, and shoring up our forces. Declan's there for now, and I know that the elemental witches are waiting. News has broken about the coven, beyond rumors. Allister is coming over as well, needing to see what magics we use so he can try to protect Europe's Packs as well."

Allister was the Alpha of the Thames Pack. He was an ally to us, and frequently flew over from outside London where his Pack was based. He had lost one of his Pack-mates here on the battlefield, and I knew it gutted him more than he let on.

We had all lost people, but that fateful day when we lost Blake and Tatiana seemed to haunt us more than most.

But I pushed those thoughts out of my mind, remembering that we had more in front of us, more loss to come. Because that was the only way that the vampires fought. By taking who we were from each other.

"We've been gone from the den for too long, so after we meet with these final two, we'll head home. It's time. And there are things that need to be discussed."

I looked at Cruz, and then at Steele's confusion, and I knew that Cruz might have told Steele some of what had happened, but he hadn't told him all.

I needed to ask what, so I wouldn't reveal anything that Cruz didn't want him to know. But from the way that Steele stared at me, I had a feeling he knew what we had been keeping secret for all these months.

That I had broken the goddess's mandate, and I didn't care. Everyone already feared my magic, why not fear this?

"Get her to bed, Cruz. She needs to rest. We'll leave in the morning, and go our separate ways. And then we'll fight. It's what we do," Jade said with a nod of her head.

I raised my brow. "I don't need to be tucked in like a child."

"I said take her to bed. Didn't I?" Jade asked, but her lips twitched into a smile, and I knew she was only putting on that air of humor to try to relieve the tension.

I blushed, I couldn't help it, and Steele just rolled his eyes before saying something about going on patrol. Sawyer followed him, as did Jade, mentioning that she wanted to shore up the wards.

It seemed we'd be staying the night, at least Cruz and I would, and there was no fighting it. I wasn't an idiot, I wasn't going to try to sneak out and try to fight on my own. I would rest, or wait, and figure out exactly what the hell I was doing.

"Come on, let's get you to bed."

I just shook my head. "I'm not tired."

"Then let me tuck you in. Because my wolf needs to protect you, so just let it happen."

"Only your wolf?" I whispered, and he met my gaze, and I knew he didn't want to answer.

I wasn't even sure I wanted him to.

So I held out my hand and let him lift me off the couch. And then without thinking, I leaned my head against his shoulder and he picked me up, carrying me towards the small guest bedroom that Jade had allocated for us.

It was odd, to let someone hold me like this, to let Cruz hold me like this. I never leaned on others if I could help it. I needed to be strong, I needed to show that the magic I held was under control so the Pack wouldn't fear what was to come.

I didn't want Cruz to think I was weak, and yet at the same time I knew it could be different with him. I knew I could rest and he would allow it.

Or maybe he would be the one to force it.

"You've already showered to get the blood off, but do you want a bath?"

I shook my head, knowing he could feel the movement, before I patted his shoulder and he let me down.

"I'm fine. Did you holding me like that help your wolf?" I asked.

"Yes, and you know it did. Did it help the magic?"

"It had nothing to do with magic, Cruz. I'm fine now. I promise you."

He cupped my face, his thumb running along my cheekbone. "I want to believe that. But you were broken in front of me. And it was only Jade's healing that brought you back."

"I had a cut on my head, and on my side, and they're both healed up. I'm not even sore. My headache that came from using magic against her is gone too."

Cruz froze. "Her?" he asked, gaze alert.

I blinked, confused. "I don't know why I said that, but it feels like it was a her. I should know, but I don't. And that confuses me. I don't know what it means, or what we need to do, but we'll have to think on it."

"Not tonight. Tonight, you're going to bed."

"I'm not tired."

"You should be. You were attacked, we've been hunting for your friends for days now, and you've barely gotten any sleep."

My lips twitched even though they shouldn't. "Probably because the nights that we haven't been on the run or fighting, we've been in bed. Together."

In an instant Cruz changed, his eyes glowing gold as he stared at me. "Get into bed, Dara."

This was all kinds of wrong. We didn't have time for this, and yet we needed to make time. I had a horrible feeling that there wouldn't be much time after this. So I raised my chin and smiled, letting my powers seep out little by little, letting control not be the first thing on my mind. I wouldn't hurt him, I couldn't. At least not this way.

"What if I say no?"

"Dara."

One word, a growl, a warning.

"What if I say no?"

And then Cruz's mouth was on mine, and I clung to him, needing him.

I had almost lost him, I knew that. Just like he had almost lost me, but I pushed that from my mind. I just wanted to believe—in this moment, in him.

Because there was a reason we were potentials, a reason fate had put us together, and it wasn't just who we could be. It was that attraction, that need.

Because I wanted Cruz beyond all reason, even if I knew it was a mistake.

This could be a mistake but I wasn't going to let it be. Instead, I kept kissing him, roaming my hands over his body as he continued to explore my mouth, his own hands on my hips, gripping tightly. He would leave bruises, but I wanted those reminders.

I wanted him, and I couldn't hold back. I wouldn't. Not in this moment. Because this moment was just for us.

He gently pushed me towards the bed, and I let him, scraping my nails down his back. I pulled off his leather jacket, as he did the same to my cardigan, and then he was plucking at the buttons of my blouse, gently but quickly, with a firm touch as if he knew exactly what he was doing. And as I'd had his hands on me before, I knew he did. I pulled on the bottom of his shirt, and he stepped back, pulling his shirt over his head in one movement, in the sexiest move I had ever seen in my life. I licked my lips, my mouth going suddenly dry at the sight of him. Shirtless, all hard muscle and scars. He was mine, if only for this night.

I leaned forward and pressed my lips over his heart. He shuddered, and then we were tangled on the bed. We pulled at each other's pants, laughing roughly as we tripped over each other, but it didn't matter. I just wanted him. I wanted to just *be*.

When his hand slid between my legs, finding me wet, I groaned.

"Cruz, I need you."

"Patience, my witch. Patience." He slid one finger deep inside me, my body clenching around him. I shifted on him, rocking my hips on his hand as I tried to come, but he wouldn't let me. He pressed his thumb along my clit, rubbing softly, then harder, just the right motions to nearly get me off, but would stop before I could get there.

I growled in frustration, but then he lowered his lips to my breasts, sucking one nipple, then the other. I wanted more, needed more. When he inserted a second finger, I couldn't hold back. I came, drenching his hand as I shook, my body warming, my nipples hardening. He took my mouth with his, capturing me with each breath, each motion.

I wiggled down, grateful when he let go of me for an instant, and then he was on his back, and I was between his legs.

"I thought I was supposed to be the one taking care of you."

I looked up at him then, his cock in my hand. He was long, thick, and I could barely put my middle finger and thumb together as I circled him. "Let me take care of you. Just for tonight."

"Whatever you say, witch," he said, as he slid his hand through my hair, then his thumb along my jaw. I looked up at him, but I didn't want the seriousness of who we were to settle into this, so I licked the tip of his cock, the pre-come salty on my tongue. He groaned, his head rolling back as I swallowed him whole, my tongue laving against the deep and ruddy vein at the bottom of his dick. It looked as if he was straining not to fuck my mouth, so I continued to go down on him, hollowing my cheeks, and then letting my throat relax slightly so I could take him deeper, the tip of his cock touching the back of my throat. I hummed and he growled, pulling back before I could do much more than cup his balls.

"No, ride my face."

"You ask the prettiest things." We twisted so I was still sucking him down, but he had his hands on my ass, spreading my cheeks as he licked and sucked at my clit, my pussy, and more. He continued to play, teasing both entrances, before sucking on my clit hard and spreading me even more, and I was coming, riding his face with abandon, as he nearly rocked off the bed, his hips shaking.

"You taste like sweet honey, and I want more."

The magic in the room throbbed, rising with each thrust, and I knew that if we weren't careful, we would light up the entire house between the two of us. We might not be bonded in the traditional way, but there was something there, and we were feeding off each other, not taking, but giving, and it was everything I never knew I needed.

When he moved me to all fours, my body weak, I looked over my shoulder at him and smiled, reveling that we were taking a moment just for us, even if we didn't have that moment to give. He grabbed my hips and thrust into me in one swift and solid movement, and I came. Just like that, I came again, and he hadn't even teased me.

He smiled, looking far too prideful, so I slammed back onto him, fucking him hard just as he did the same to me. And then we were moving, him going deeper than before, and I couldn't breathe, couldn't think. When we rolled so I was on top of him, riding him, he had his hands on my breasts, his eyes bright gold. We didn't need lights in the room, not with my magic and his eyes.

And the tattered bond between us wove together just a bit tighter, not enough, because it wasn't a mating bond, it was something else, but it was ours.

Even if I knew it was only the beginning. Or perhaps our ending. When he came, he roared my name and I fell on top of him, spent, sweaty, and his. I clung to him, ignoring the tears sliding down my cheeks.

He kissed them away, holding me.

I knew this couldn't be forever.

Not with a prophecy, not with me bringing him back.

This wasn't our forever, it couldn't be.

I hated myself, and I hated fate.

Because I wanted him. I did the one thing I told myself I wouldn't do, I wanted Cruz.

And I couldn't have him. So I wept, and let him hold me.

CHAPTER THIRTEEN

Dara

THE NEXT MORNING, BY THE TIME STEELE, JADE, AND Sawyer were on their way out, my nerves were on edge.

I knew they needed to go, that we needed to begin the process of blending magics to protect us, but it was hard to see them go. I wanted them to be safe, and being near us wouldn't allow that. They would be safer away from us, and not actually in the war zone.

"Do you think that whoever is attacking us is following us?"

"You and Jade put up new wards, the personal ones to keep vampires out. We have to hope it's enough. At least for now."

"I'm just afraid it won't be. And I know that's pessimistic of me, but I don't know what else to think."

He reached out and gripped my hand, and I didn't even think he realized he was doing it until he was holding me, but I wasn't going to push him away. Not when the taste of last night was still on my tongue.

I hadn't gotten much sleep, and I know that was my own fault. But I didn't care. I couldn't, when I had a feeling that might have been the last time I would share a bed with him. Because after this we'd be going home, to a place where we needed to protect our den, and we couldn't worry about silly things like bonds slowly killing us and mating bonds that could never appear.

"They're warning the Pack that we're getting things ready. We'll do what we can. Now, who are we finding?"

"It took a while to find them because they've been hidden, we're going to Bishop first. His place is on the other side of the city, and he doesn't know we're coming, so he isn't going to be happy."

"Who is Bishop?"

"He's a psychic. A mental mage."

Cruz nearly drove off the road and stared at me for an instant before putting his eyes back on the scene in front of him.

"Are you serious?"

"I am. He doesn't use it often how you're thinking, but he can. It hurts him. He also makes really good potions. That's what he's best at. You think my magic room looks like it's full of herbs and magical items, but it's nothing compared to his. At least that's how he used to be, and

Jade says he's only gotten more talented and a little more hoarder-ish."

"Is hoarder-ish a word?" he asked.

"Probably not, but I'm going with it. His powers are not elements. Just like mine aren't."

"Jade's the only one so far that seems to be elemental, though I have a feeling there's something that lies beneath that surface."

"It's not my secret to share." And I wasn't even sure I knew the full scope of her powers.

"And metal is an element, just not the ones that you usually think of when it comes to witch powers," Cruz said far more calmly than I thought he would when mentioning Declan. However, I was in Cruz's bed last night, not Declan's, so maybe that's why he could. And Declan was far away.

"We're going to ask Bishop to help us. And you need him?"

"We need his expansive knowledge. I think we're running out of time. The attacks? They're following us. Maybe not right now, but they have been. And we need a way to stop the vampires from slicing into us."

"You found an antidote to the jagged shards of magic that slam into us and affect our shifting."

"But we haven't found a way to stop hybrids from happening, or for a way to find control. We haven't found a way to stop them from hurting our wards without having to go through me. And I don't know how much longer I have."

I shut my mouth quickly, afraid that the words had even come out at all. I hadn't meant to say them, and when he glared at me, I swallowed back my fear and told myself it was fine. It would all be fine.

Even though that was a total lie.

"Okay, I don't like the sound of that."

"I don't either, but we're almost there."

"Fine," he growled, and I knew this wasn't the end of it. It couldn't be.

We pulled into a small neighborhood, one that didn't seem like it would house a witch, not with the cookie cutter houses, and children's bikes left haphazardly in the yard, no fear that they would ever be stolen. Cruz tilted his head and sniffed as we walked up onto the sidewalk.

"Are there shifters here?"

"Some. Not our Pack, maybe one of the others. Perhaps the Centrals. We're closer to their territory here."

"Is it okay that we're here then?" I asked. I hadn't even thought about the other Packs, other territories.

When Cruz nodded, I relaxed marginally, but not entirely because we were still on a witch's territory, even if it wasn't that of a Pack.

"The cities are neutral ground, at least for us. We don't know where the vampires are, and if you say this is Bishop's neighborhood, is this his territory then? Is that how witches work?"

"Not necessarily, but Bishop is, well...unique."

I wasn't quite sure what else to say to that, but then a man with dark hair, silver at the temples, and a broad chest, narrow waist, and all muscle glared at us from his porch.

"Well, I was wondering how long it would take you to get here. Seems you went to Declan first. They always go to Declan first. Come on in. We don't have much time." I was grateful for the wards that I had put up between us. It protected our thoughts, at least I hoped it did. Bishop seemed to have grown stronger in his magic, just like I had. For all I knew he was listening in.

"Am I supposed to be singing 'Mary Had a Little Lamb' in the back of my head the whole day?" Cruz asked, and I nearly laughed despite the fact that there was nothing funny about this situation.

"No, not at all. He'd be able to get through that. And you would just annoy him. Let's not annoy him."

"Are you coming in or not, wolf? Come in, Dara. You can leave the little mutt behind."

Cruz stiffened and growled low. He didn't let his eyes go gold, because the human was in the forefront, not the wolf.

"Bishop, we're here for your hospitality. There's no need for you to be rude."

"You're here for hospitality. Well, seems I've been lacking. Welcome to my humble abode, witch and wolf.

You may enter, but if you touch anything that is mine, I will rip your heart out."

"This is supposed to be our ally?"

Someone moved from behind Bishop, and I nearly fell to my knees at the sight of her. My own powers yearned.

Her long white hair was tied back in a braid long enough to flow over her shoulder. She had kind eyes with crow's feet and lines around her mouth that hinted of smiles and strain in equal measure. Leta was seventy years old if I did my math right. Ten years younger than Cruz.

But witches and humans didn't have long lives. Unless witches bound themselves to a mate, they didn't live hundreds of years. Humans had to shift, had to be turned, violently and near death, in order to become a shifter and have their lives be extended. Humans, unless there was a shock of fate and other powers involved, didn't end up with a mate's long life. There needed to be some intervention.

Leta had lived her life, and now was here, standing behind Bishop, and from the look on her face was ready to fight for us. Beside us.

I didn't understand fate sometimes. Leta was seventy years old, younger than Cruz, and yet Cruz looked as if he were maybe thirty. What goddesses let that happen? What goddesses let dark magic into the world in which it corrupted us? None of us had asked for this. None of us had chosen our fates.

But I still didn't understand the undeserved cruelty of

it all. The human government, and the humans' population, knew that wolves were long lived. They had taken most of it in stride, thinking of the fantastical ways that they had heard about shifters and now vampires in stories and myths.

I knew that there had to be experiments, cruelties beyond measure, performed on shifters in order to find that longevity, to find the path to immortality. There always would be. There had been sacrifices within the witches' community in the past, beyond the Salem witch trials in order to create immortality. It had never worked, because darkness always corrupted. I was not darkness. I was death, but death was a part of life. Even those with near immortality died. That was why we fought as a Pack for each other. I did not have a long life in front of me. I had known that long before I met Cruz. Because of my powers, because of the way I touched death, I knew I wouldn't live to even Leta's age.

I might have had a chance if I had bonded with Cruz the right way, but I hadn't. And I wouldn't.

Because we were already dying with each other.

No. I refused to allow Cruz to die for me.

Not when I already saved him once.

"Are you going to stand there, child? You should come in. I've made tea. And I did it, not the little potion master next to me. I promise it's safe."

"I would never poison someone in my own home. It's

gauche," Bishop snarled, before he slammed the door behind us after we entered.

"What are the two of you doing here together? I've been searching for you both, and I didn't realize you would be in the same house."

Bishop opened his mouth, probably to say something rude towards Cruz, but Leta held up her hand. She was a strong witch, though not as strong as the rest of us. But because of her years, and her kindness even in the face of war and pain, we listened when she spoke.

"We knew we must quicken the journey because the moon goddess spoke to us. So I came to Bishop and got through his annoying tendencies. And when the time comes, we will go with you to your den."

"Yes, because we need to protect the cute little wolves. The little baby pups who can't even protect themselves."

Before I could blink, Bishop's back was against the wall and Cruz had his hand around Bishop's throat. "Did you just threaten the pups of the den?" Cruz asked.

"Well, we see we act with violence first. Shifters haven't changed much, have they?"

"Cruz, don't kill him. We need him."

"I can mar him a bit. A little maiming."

Leta laughed out loud.

"I like him. Bishop, stop being an asshole. You're fine. And you did mention pups. We do not hurt the young and innocent."

"I said pups because I was trying to be derogatory

towards the wolf in front of me. I apologize. I don't hurt children."

"Use better terms then. Mutt worked fine earlier. That's better than threatening to harm a child."

Bishop held both hands up and narrowed his eyes.

"Nice magic wards to keep me out of your thoughts. It'll work for now, I can help you with a few tricks to help more. I don't want your thoughts, wolf. Nor do I want yours, Dara. I use my powers in order to attack, but only if I have to. I can use it against your vampires. But only if your wolf lets me go."

I saw Cruz tighten his grip for an instant before he stepped back.

"Why do you hate us so much?"

Bishop laughed, before lifting up his shirt. Along his lean muscles, I saw the claw marks. Three slashes that had to have been made by a wolf's claws.

Cruz looked at them and cursed under his breath. "What happened?"

"A rogue. A wolf that couldn't hold his own, and then didn't turn me. I ended up a bleeding mess, and the witches that were helping me at the time didn't care much. They left me to die."

"What happened to the rogue?" Cruz asked.

"He died. Killed by one of your trackers. I don't know which Pack and I don't care anymore. I'll protect the wolves because I do want to protect those pups. I apologize for using that word."

"And I apologize that we couldn't stop the rogue before it hurt you. We've had issues with the vampires, with the way that other powers have tried to push rogues at us. We're finding a way to protect them. To bring them back."

I turned to Cruz, eyes wide. "What?"

"Yes, one of the Redwoods and Talon Pack members figured out a way. Not for all of them, but for some. I'm sorry that we missed this one. That you were hurt. But it wasn't me, so you don't have to try to claw off my face because I'm standing in the same room with you. And you're lucky I have the control that I do."

"Did you just threaten me at the same time as apologizing?" Bishop asked.

"You are one who just said you use your magic to hurt others and to protect. I do the same. But I know from the witches in my life that you are controlling something else within you. That is what a shifter does. And sometimes there's a pull the other way that breaks that connection between you and the control that you have and you turn. I'm sorry you were hurt, but it wasn't me, so let's fix this. Let's stand united, help the witches, help the shifters, and get the demons controlling these vampires."

"Demons, it always comes back to demons," Leta said with a sigh. She held her hands out, the scars on them evident. "Did you know that blood working began long before the idea of shifters and magic?"

Cruz turned, eyes wide, and I knew I should have mentioned this.

"Leta is a blood witch."

When the man who could have been my mate frowned, I held up a hand. But it was Leta who answered. "I use my own blood as much as possible." She pulled up her sleeves, showing the scars on her body. "I use my own when I can, and sometimes the scars don't go away. If I can't use my own, I use blood that is freely given. I don't kill, I don't maim. Not unless I'm forced to. But there's something you need to know before we go."

"We already know that there's a demon in charge, one that came back through the veil."

"I know you do. And that's how vampires were made in the past. I cannot use the blood of the dead for my magic. And yet I've used vampire blood before to control, to create the magic needed."

I froze, my eyes widening. "The vampires, they're turned humans. They're dead. Aren't they?"

"They have to be. They're not who they were before they turned."

Leta looked between us and shook her head. "That's not all of it. It's been how many years since the demon first walked onto this plane and changed the way that our society runs? They may have done it in the past, but vampires have been here for a while now. They've changed. Because I can use their blood, they have to be alive." The older woman sighed. "And they're the ones that protected me."

I took a step forward, hand outstretched. "What are you talking about? Vampires protected you?"

She nodded tightly. "Why do you think that the only ones out there are bad? Why do you think that the only vampires that exist are the ones that are trying to get you? Witches and shifters have lived in secret for so long that we have forgotten when shifters were first made, that it was a punishment from the moon goddess. A punishment which is to be in the darkness, and the light. Why can't vampires be the same?"

"Are you telling me that there are good vampires out there that can be our allies?" Cruz asked.

Leta met his gaze and then mine. "I'm telling you that a group of vampires saved my life from a roaming horde before they disappeared. I don't know who they were, but they are out there. And I can use their blood in my magics. They might be turned, but perhaps if they have control, and aren't being controlled, there may be a way to make them allies."

I shook my head, the revelations too much. "We need to focus on building this coven. We need to find a way to protect our Pack."

"And we will. We will protect who we can. But there are others out there. And I think that might be a place to start. Or at least a place to find a bridge, because I don't know what's coming, and in my long years I have seen too much. Too much darkness, too much death.

"But I've also seen that for those who reach out, for those who find allies, they are the strongest. Our coven, the one we make, the one we use to create magics that have never been made before, *that* will be strong. For I have seen it. But that can't be the only step taken.

"There are forces coming, forces we don't yet know. And you know the prophecy, the one for you, just like I've seen the one for me. I need to bring back those who are lost.

"There will be pain and suffering along the way. But perhaps there can be hope. Perhaps it isn't just black and white, light and dark. Perhaps there's something else in between."

I looked at Cruz, and wondered exactly what the hell that meant.

CHAPTER

FOURTEEN

Cruz

By the time we got back to the den later that night, it felt as if the world had shifted, and I was just trying to keep up.

Well, I wasn't sure I could even do that. I would try, but it wouldn't be easy.

"We're meeting with the others, right? Introducing the witches to them, and then going over everything."

I turned to Dara as we stood outside of her home, and I noticed the dark circles under her eyes. She had been tired this entire trip but had persevered. And yet as soon as we had gotten back to the den, as soon as the wards had increased in strength in her presence, she had gotten more tired.

It wasn't just me that was killing her, it was all of us. And we needed to change that. Because I wasn't going to be able to survive without her, and I didn't know when that had happened. I didn't know how we were supposed to change it.

But I would fight for her because she was here.

"We're going to tell them everything."

Dara's eyes widened. "What do you mean everything?"

"I told Steele. About the battle. About the bond."

Dara took a step back, her hand gripping the porch rail behind her. "That's why he looked at me like that. Because he knows that I'm killing you."

I growled low and stepped forward. My hands were on her, cupping her cheeks, then moving down to hold her shoulders, bracing her.

"No. He didn't look at you that way because he thinks you're killing me. You aren't."

"I am. Every time I have to use magic, I take from you."

"I'm the fucking leech. I'm the one taking from you. But we're going to fix that. Because I'll be damned if we let this continue. He wasn't looking at you for any other reason other than he's worried for you, just like I am. He doesn't hate you. He doesn't blame you. You saved my life, Dara. And you are my fucking mate. There's nothing that could be wrong with that."

"There are more important things than how I feel right now. We have so much to do."

"And we'll deal with it. I'm going to tell them about Blade. About what Jade said."

And then it wasn't me comforting her, but Dara's hand on my chest, feeling my heartbeat. I loved when she did that, it was as if it connected my wolf to her magic. She couldn't shift, would never be a shifter. She wouldn't need to go through that. She had her own power, something that my wolf yearned to connect with beyond how it already was.

I wanted more. I needed it.

"I'm going to tell them, and they're going to know everything. The problem with Blade is that he kept secrets, and we can't do that."

"Good. They're not going to blame you. They don't blame Chase. And you've spent years trying to ensure that Chase knew his worth. Now he can do the same for you, just like I will."

"Well, that will be one worry that we have to deal with. Just like our mating bond."

"Cruz." Pain slid over her face, but she didn't say anything else.

"I can't go back to the way that things were before. When we were fighting and pushing at each other and not talking about what was important. We just said that we couldn't keep secrets, they couldn't prevail. So I'm not going back to that."

"Cruz, we have to build the coven, fight against the vampires. We have to figure out how they were following us. And who this light magic user is. We need to figure all this out. I'm fine. We don't have time to go into anything more."

I knew she was talking out of fear, so I let her, even though it wasn't easy. Even though I wanted to shout at her for not putting herself first for once.

"I can't. We can't. Not with what happened. We might not have the mating bond, but fuck it. I'm done. I'm done with everything changing around us and not giving us a second to just breathe. We're not going to go back to how it was. We're going to find our own way, together. Because I am done watching you fade away to protect us while there's nothing I can do. You want to stand by my side when I tell the people that everything I have known my entire life was a lie? Then do it as the woman who could be my mate. And we'll fix that too. I am done fighting with no results."

She let out a hollow laugh, and I had no idea how to take that.

"I don't think we can, Cruz. I feel like we've been heading down this path for a long while."

I hated the fact that it sounded as if she were waiting for an ending. Waiting for *her* ending.

I would be damned if I allowed that to happen.

I leaned forward and crushed my mouth to hers. She

leaned into me, her nails digging into my chest. She wouldn't leave a mark, but I would feel it nonetheless.

"If you two are done, we have a meeting to go to," Steele growled from beside us. I had scented him coming up of course, but my wolf had ignored him. He was an ally, a friend, and a pain in my ass.

"I'm busy," I mumbled against Dara's lips, and she laughed.

She laughed.

She didn't do that enough, and I would do whatever I could to make sure that she did that more often.

Even if I was so damn afraid that we were running out of time.

"Chase and the others are waiting. We've got to go."

I pulled away and held out my hand. "Stand by my side?"

"Cruz. You don't need to do this."

"I'll be damned if I go in without my mate by my side. I don't fucking care if we don't have a mating bond. But we chose each other. Fate may have pushed us together, but we're choosing each other."

We might not have had time to figure out our feelings, or tell each other exactly what we meant, but I wasn't going to let her do this alone.

When she slid her hand into mine, I let out a relieved breath, squeezed her hand, and made my way to my Alpha's house.

Steele looked between us, curiosity and worry mixed

in his gaze. My best friend of course would be worried about this.

By the time we were sitting in the Alpha's home, everyone had already noticed our hands—the way we were touching, and there was confusion in their gazes.

Because there was no bond, and this wasn't just a casual dalliance. Not with the way that we were during an Alpha Pack meeting.

"You're back. I heard there was trouble," Chase said. "And I'm sorry for it. I'm sorry we didn't send Steele with you in the first place. Are you sure you're okay, Dara?" he asked, his gaze intent.

Dara nodded beside me, then looked down at her hands. "I don't know who that witch was. Her power was immense though, and it was stolen. She's siphoning powers and I want to know how she's doing it."

"Do you think the coven will be able to help?" Audrey asked, standing next to her mate. Gavin looked between Dara and me, a brow raised, before he nudged his mate's shoulder.

"I think the coven will be able to do much good, but it's going to take them time. So we need to also rely on our own powers. I've been tracking what I can, but they're hiding their tracks well."

Gavin was the Tracker of the Pack, and not just with his senses as wolf, but with goddess-bound powers. He could find anyone, as long as magic didn't disrupt it, which was coming up more and more frequently as this war continued.

It wasn't just wolf against wolf, we were fighting against the government, the vampires, witches, humans, and the unknown. And it was the last one that worried me more than anything.

Because whoever was orchestrating this, that master, "that demon" as Valac had put it, told me that this was an ending. One I didn't want to consider.

One I didn't think I would have a choice but to face one day.

"Tell us what happened. Everything. In detail," Cassius said, and I wasn't surprised to see him here, even if he wasn't part of the Pack hierarchy.

We would be meeting with the other Alphas, and other Packs soon. And not just the council, but those in our alliance. I knew Allister was staying with the Talon Pack right now, having come over from England, so he would be there too. But for now we were starting small and working our way out. It would take endless meetings to make sure everyone knew the information they needed to.

Audrey as our Beta was here with her mate, as was our Alpha, Skye sitting next to him, looking exhausted as well.

She had been running back and forth between the Packs, trying to ensure that we were all trained in keeping up with the powers that were coming at us.

It was odd for Adalyn not to be here, as she had always

been in our Pack meetings, but she was recently mated with two mates, in the Alpha structure of the Central Pack, and pregnant.

Steele was in the room, glaring at us, mostly because he knew what was coming. At least part of it.

Wren stood quietly in the corner, next to Hayes. While Wren couldn't feel the emotions in the room, she was still a submissive lynx, and so many dominants in a room was hard for her. Hayes on the other hand, was a dominant polar bear, but as Omega, could sense every emotion not locked down tightly. I didn't know how he could take it. I had enough issues with the Pack bonds as Heir. I didn't know how he did it.

While Cassius was there because he trained with all of us, and could fight vampires like nobody's business, neither Novah nor Wynter were in the room, which surprised me. Novah was a truth seeker. She could tell if someone was telling the truth, and lies hurt her. I didn't know why she wasn't here, because she was usually present for big meetings, especially with outside people present. And though Wynter was human, she was a fighter, and had been present at the start of all of this, and was the reason why we had even gone on this trip to begin with. I would ask why later. Because for now I just wanted to get everything out there.

"The people who I think will make a good balance for the coven, and not exclusively elemental witches, are waiting to come inside. I want you guys to meet them if possible." Dara looked between us. "I know this is asking you to have a lot of faith in us, but I think it's important."

"I think that the coven doesn't have to be part of the Pack," Chase said slowly, as if sounding out his words. "They need to be a separate entity, but connected, just like each Pack is under the alliance. It is not our say who becomes coven. It's yours, Dara. It's those who can come together and create this magic. So we don't get to be the ones to vet these witches." I growled a bit, as did Steele and the others. But Chase held up his hands. "While I would love to be able to play a nice chess game and put everybody where I think they need to be, I can't. That's for the goddesses. And the gods. That's not for me. That's not for us."

Dara let out a weak laugh, and I looked over at her. "All we do is try to put people where they go, and nothing's ever working. But the magical users in this alliance, and those surrounding it, need help. They need a connection, a base. That's why I'm doing this. That, and our Pack needs us. They need the magic users, just like the magic users need the shifters. It's a symbiotic balance that we have not had for far too long. Even the Packs who haven't had dark magic enter their lives need them. And they haven't had them since the coven changed a few years ago. These people, who were my friends and are my friends, and though we lost Iris along the way," she said, her voice breaking, "we can work together. So yes, I want you to meet them."

"Of course I will. And we're going to help as much as we can, and I hope they can help us."

"There are a few other things," I said, looking at Dara who nodded, then at Steele. "First, I need to tell you all about the bond."

Audrey moved forward, her eyes wide, but I held out my hand. "It's not a mating bond." I explained it, about my death and subsequent resurrection. Skye wiped tears from her eyes, and Chase began to pace.

"You did this and you didn't ask for help?" Wren asked, coming towards Dara.

"Who was I supposed to ask? What other witch can do this?"

"I don't know. But you could have told us."

Dara wiped tears of her own away. "I didn't want to worry you."

"Of course we've been worried," Audrey snapped. "You've been hurting and we haven't been able to help."

"You've always helped. You've been by my side every time we've made a breakthrough against the vampires. You've always been there. And you will be. But now you know the truth of it. And it wasn't all my story to tell. It was Cruz's, too."

I turned to her and gripped her hand. "And now we know and we're going to fix this."

She gave me a sad smile and I knew she didn't believe me, but dammit, we would fix it.

"That's a whole hell of a lot. What else did we miss?"

I swallowed hard, knowing that there were more than a few things. But, I would start with the easiest. Or rather, the easiest for me.

"You're going to meet Leta, a blood witch."

"Do you mind telling me what that means?" Steele asked. "I missed that part when I was escorting the fire witch and her little friend here."

I ignored the barb at both Jade and Sawyer, because Steele had his own reasons for his reaction.

"It's something you're going to have to ask her. But Dara trusts her, and so do I."

"Well, I like the sound of that," Audrey said. "Why are you bringing Leta up when we're going to meet her soon?" my Beta asked.

"Because she mentioned something about vampires." I let out a breath, and was grateful when Dara continued.

"She said that a group of vampires saved her from the horde. Ones that had full control over their faculties, full control of their powers. And they chose to help rather than harm."

Everyone began speaking at once, asking questions we didn't have answers to, but when our Alpha held up his hand, everyone quieted, the dominance in his tone soothing my wolf even as it terrified it.

"Are you telling me that there are good vampires out there?"

"I'm telling you there might be. And we could find allies."

Steele grumbled, but I ignored him, looking directly at Chase. "That's not all."

My Alpha ran his hands through his hair and began to pace. "So far you've told us that you've come back from the dead, there might be good vampires out there, and that magic could destroy or save us all. What else did you learn in the four days you were away from this fucking den?"

I still couldn't believe that everything had happened in such a short period, but then again we had been leading up to this for years. Dara and I had been circling each other, and this wasn't just about her, it wasn't just about me. I looked around this room, and I trusted every single person here.

I could have pulled Chase to the side, and brought Skye with him because he would always tell his mate everything. But I didn't want secrets anymore. So I stood up and met my Alpha's gaze for an instant before lowering my eyes. Dara slid her hand into mine, and just like that, that bond that wasn't a bond pulsed between us, and I let out a breath.

"Dara and the others are going to have to clean up the spell, but there is one more thing you need to know."

"Spell?" Skye asked, her voice soft as she stood by her mate.

Chase froze and looked directly at me. I didn't need to lower my gaze, not right then. Because I wasn't looking at my Alpha just then.

He was a confused little boy, just like I had been.

"What are you talking about, Cruz?"

"Blade used dark magic, we think, to change the rules of mating. He hid who he was to me, who I was to this Pack. I didn't come to this Pack later on in life, I wasn't pulled away from my mother because she wanted to be a lone wolf. Everything that I thought was a lie. She had been Aspen. Before. And when Blade wanted another child, he made one."

Unlike before, nobody made a sound, I didn't think anyone could.

"He made *me*. Blade was my father. That's why I'm the Heir of this Pack. And I have no idea what the hell that means. But the time for secrets is done. Our past keeps hitting us right in the face, and if we're going to go headlong into this future, we're going to have to brace for it. So, Chase, it turns out, I'm your brother."

Chase stared at me, eyes wide, when someone cleared their throat from the doorway.

Novah, our truth seeker and Cassius' mate, stood in the doorway, her eyes filled with tears as she put her hands over her lips.

"Truth. That's the truth, and I think the spell's finally breaking. I think the spells from Blade's past are finally breaking."

I turned to Chase, and he just shook his head. My wolf lowered its head in submission, disappointment. But then Chase's arms were around me, hugging me close.

"I fucking knew it. Somehow I fucking knew it. Welcome home, little brother. It's about damn time."

People came forward, hugging us, speaking over each other, and I knew this was only the beginning. It had to be.

We hadn't solved anything, we had just broken through a few secrets.

The hard part was yet to come.

But this time we would be ready. We had to be.

CHAPTER FIFTEEN

Lily

Lily paced the small room, frowning. Things were going her way. She had killed that witch, had sent out more of her kind. But it wasn't enough.

Dara had escaped, and she hadn't been able to siphon enough magic. That fucking witch would soon learn the truth of who she was. Lily would need to stop that. To take away whatever the hell that Dara thought she had within her.

This had been a long time coming, and soon they would realize who was the strongest all along.

"Miss Lily," a voice said, and she turned to see Matthew, the human in charge of HOG. Lily wanted to roll her eyes, but she needed Matthew and what he represented.

"You're here. Finally."

"I'm sorry it took so long. But we're ready. We're standing with the others, to ensure that we can surround this Pack. They're so busy worrying about each other, they don't see us." Matthew frowned. "They never see us."

Lily moved forward and cupped his face. "I understand, darling. But I see you. Soon we will surround them, and they won't know what hit them. You will protect all of us. I know you will."

Matthew lowered his head and kissed her forehead. When he stepped back, Lily grinned. "Thank you. For everything."

"It's okay, Lily. These abominations, these monsters, think that they can rule us. But they can't. Soon they'll learn who their betters are. That they should have been paying attention to us all along."

He saluted her, as if she cared about any of that, and he turned to go back to his people.

The sound of a slow clap hit her ears and she whirled to see Malphas. Her consort, her demon.

He smiled at her, his grin wide, his dark hair pulled back from his face in a tight queue.

"Lilith."

"Darling!" she called out and ran towards him. When she threw her hands around his neck, he caught her, twirling her. His claws dug into her flesh. The sting, painful, but needed. Blood scented the air, her blood, and she sighed as he dipped his fangs into her neck, sucking slightly. She nearly orgasmed at the feel of him feeding off of her, and she wrapped her legs around his waist, holding him close.

When he licked the wounds closed, she sighed into him.

"I've been waiting for you."

"Not waiting for too long, not with that Matthew."

Lily rolled her eyes and hugged him close. "He's just a means to an end. He'll see exactly what he's in for when he understands who he's fighting alongside."

Malphas grinned and set her down. "Good. The vampires in command are waiting for your next move."

Lily rolled her shoulders back. "I've been preparing. We have the people in place, and soon the Aspens will scream. And bleed."

"And the witch?"

Lily pushed back that sense of foreboding, the way that he said 'witch.' "You'll have her. Her blood at least."

"Good. We need her."

"You don't need her. Not really. Do you?" Lily asked, trying not to sound petulant.

Malphas slid his hand around her throat, squeezing gently before running his thumb along her lips. "Not in the way that you think, my consort. But her magic will let us open the portal to death. We need that power. It'll help our vampires, and bring forth the other demons."

"And what of the other witches that she's managed to piece together in this new coven?" Lily spat.

"You can have their magic, and you'll be the most powerful of them all."

Lily grinned, smiling. "Good. Soon they will realize that I was never the weak witch that they thought I was. They looked down on me, felt sorry for me. But all along I was with you. And they never knew."

"The Aspen Pack doesn't know a lot of things. But soon they'll figure it out, my love. Now, let's finish planning, because the den has been quiet for too long. And they must learn that though they thought they could win against the vampires, they can't win against their own memories."

Lily slid her hand into her consort's, and they walked towards the center of the room, knowing what was needed.

The Aspens would scream, would beg.

And they would lose.

Just as their goddess had wished.

CHAPTER SIXTEEN

Dara

I STOOD ON THE PORCH, MY HANDS OVER MY CHEST AS I looked out into the forest, waiting. He would be here, soon.

"I've never actually seen a shifter change. It should be interesting."

I narrowed my gaze at Declan and his far too curious tone. "No, that's not what we're going to do. You're not going to watch because it's not needed. You aren't part of this."

"Protecting your wolf then?"

"Just like he protects me, Declan." I let out a breath. "There's no need for you to act as if you care. Or be jealous. We were never much more than a fling, a way to stay warm on cold nights."

Declan's eyes widened, he put his hand over his chest, and backed up two spaces, making sure to exaggerate every movement.

"I am shocked. Shocked you would say that. You were the love of my life."

A snort sounded from behind us, and I looked to see Leta coming towards us, shaking her head. She had pulled her beautiful white hair back into a bun, and I knew she would probably let it go, so the wind could fly through the strands as we worked our magic soon.

If I were able to age, to make it to her age, I would want to look like her. And not just in her beauty, but in the way that she held herself. She was so damn strong, and I was only a little jealous.

"You're ridiculous, little boy," Leta said and he shook his head, before he put his arm around her.

"You call me little boy, old lady, and I don't appreciate it."

"You let him talk to you like that? You never let me talk to you like that," Bishop said as he came forward, Jade and Sawyer following.

They had all piled into my house as guests to the den. I hadn't been sure that Chase would let them into the den at all, not with the worry about strangers coming onto their land, but they needed the protection of the wards that we had, and Novah had taken each of them in hand, using her truth-seeking abilities in a way that I knew she didn't like.

To my surprise, none of my friends had argued. They had listened, answered questions, and made sure that they proved to be as trustworthy as possible.

They knew the gravity of this decision, of what we needed to do, and they weren't going to risk it.

Not even Declan and his sarcasm. Or Bishop and the fear I knew that wafted around him every time we saw the shifters.

Later that afternoon we would take action, but it still felt as if others were watching us. Waiting. Somebody had followed us. Somebody had killed Iris, and I would find them.

I would find who had attacked us and do my best to save my people.

Before I didn't have anyone left.

"Come on, we need to head to the council area. You'll meet us there?" Jade asked and I turned.

"I thought I was coming with you."

"You are, but I think you need a little alone time with your wolf." She paused, staring off into the distance as if she saw something that we didn't. Perhaps she did. I didn't know Jade's magic. Not like I knew others, but we all hid our magics for reasons of our own.

"I think we're not going to have a lot of time to sit back and relax. Whoever came after Iris is coming after us. We need to get through this first. Go. Meet your wolf, we'll wait for you."

Leta moved forward, cupped my face. "We will fix your bond. You're too young for this, child. We'll fix this. We'll do what we should have done years ago." She kissed my cheek and left me confused. Bishop growled, while Declan looked around, as if waiting for someone to jump out and say that they shouldn't be there. Sawyer stood by quietly, the last to leave the porch.

"Are you going with them?" I asked.

"I don't like when Jade goes out alone like this. She's too busy taking care of everyone else and nobody takes care of her."

I tilted my head, studying him. "I don't know you, Sawyer. But Novah and Jade both trust you. Just take care of my friend?"

"Always." He paused. "She's just my friend, Dara. She saved me a while ago, and I promised I'd always be there for her." He looked down at his hands. "And I don't have anywhere else to go. The humans don't really have power in this. Not without bringing guns and laws into it. I'll do what I can to fight alongside Jade. And you. Because nobody deserves to live in fear."

"I'm going to have to introduce you to Dhani. She's a human who is part of our Pack, and fights at our side."

"I met her earlier. She's nice. And I'm glad that she has power here."

He left me alone on the porch, and I noticed Steele

and Hayes as well as three other soldiers following the group out.

I shook my head, but knew it was for a reason. The Pack had just completed a Pack run, many of the wolves and cats and others winding through the forest, letting their animals to the front so they could breathe.

It was a way to connect to being a shifter. I had gone a few times, to stand with the others who didn't shift. Novah was latent and didn't shift into her wolf. So I usually stood with her, as she yearned so intently that even I could feel it deep down within my own soul.

Before I could let my thoughts wander too much, a familiar wolf walked forward, and I froze, looking at the beauty of him.

He was a gray blur, but gorgeous with soft fur and gold eyes.

I loved the look of Cruz in wolf form. And now that I knew to look for it, I realized that he had the same tufts of white on his paws that Chase did.

They were brothers, and I knew we would all have to come to reconcile that with our own memories.

Without even thinking about it, I walked off the porch and towards my wolf.

Because he was mine, if only for this moment.

Cruz came up to me and sniffed at my hip, so I kneeled down and ran my hands over his fur. I had only done this in battle, never like this before. I knew the man, but now I was getting to know the wolf. His ears twitched as I rubbed between them, and then he licked my chin.

I scowled down at him.

"Oh no. Don't think you can do that again."

He did that again.

I laughed and kissed his snout. "Can you shift back? I know you must be tired after your run, but I want to meet with the others. At least get there before the Alphas do. We have a lot to prepare."

He nipped up my chin, gently, a bare brush of fang, and I shivered, knowing that I wouldn't carry his mark.

I couldn't.

He padded away, behind a bush, and I didn't watch.

I had seen him shift, seen others shift. It was a painful and personal experience, and I didn't want to have him worry about me.

Thankfully it took less than five minutes. He was getting faster, they all were. A few wolves could even shift in a blink, with immense pain, but could still do it. Cruz was getting faster, with the new magic that the moon goddess had given them all. And soon he would be able to shift as quickly as I could pull on my magic. I wanted that for him, because I had hoped it would mean less pain.

Cruz came out, naked, hard, and I swallowed.

"Oh. Well. I didn't even think about getting you clothes. I should get you clothes."

He growled, and I was grateful that I was on the edge of the den, hidden. My neighbors couldn't see me in this part of my yard, and I didn't sense any other people around me. But then again, it was hard to think with Cruz in front of me, naked, his cock tapping against his belly with each step.

"Mate, you better run. Or I'm going to take you."

I pressed my thighs together, grateful I was wearing a dress. I liked the feel of flowing fabric on my skin, it always helped when my magic was too hot, burning along my body, to have that feel. It was a texture thing, but in that moment, all I could think about was him.

"Run, mate."

Instead, I moved forward and traced my fingertips along his jaw.

"What if I don't want to?" I asked.

And then his lips were on me and he had one hand under my dress, between my legs before I could think. He speared me with two fingers, and I nearly came, shaking.

"Goddess!" I cried out, and he grinned, bit my lip.

"Be quiet, little witch. Or the others are going to hear you. You don't want them to hear you."

"Cruz. Just fuck me already. I need you."

"I've been thinking about you all day."

"Good."

When he kissed me again I groaned, and then he was pressing me back against the tree. I called out, the bark rubbing into my skin, and he pulled away, frowning.

"No, I like it. Go."

"I don't want to hurt you."

We were silent for just a bare instant, a moment when we knew that this wasn't about the heat between us, but of the moments to come. I didn't want to think about that. I couldn't. So instead I kissed him again and he groaned against me, his hand still between my legs even as he used his free hand to grip my thigh, keeping me steady in the air. My toes dangled off the ground, but it didn't matter. I just wanted him.

I slid one hand between us, gripping his cock, guiding him to my entrance.

"Please, I just want to come with you inside me."

"You say the sweetest things." And then he was deep inside me, stretching me, filling me.

I couldn't think, couldn't breathe, I just moved with him, wanting him.

My magic soared within me, along the bond that wasn't a bond, as I pulled towards him. I wanted him, but I couldn't have him. When his teeth grazed my neck, I shivered, wanting him.

"Do it. I just, I know it's not real. But do it."

I didn't even realize I was saying the words, but he heard me. He stiffened for an instant before he bit down, his fangs digging into my flesh.

In order for a mating bond to snap into place once you found your potential mate, you did two things:

For the human, you made love, you connected in the most personal and carnal way.

For the animal, the shifter marked their mate, and if

their mate was a shifter they would return the bite. He bit into my neck where it met my shoulder, and as blood seeped from the wound, he lapped it up. I knew I wouldn't scar, and the mark wouldn't be visible. But the world would know I was his. And that was all that mattered.

But since I wasn't a shifter, I didn't need to mark him.

But I wanted to.

So as I came, the mark sending me over the edge, I put my hand over his chest, and pulsed my magic. Just a little, just a touch, but I knew he would be marked by me, even if we couldn't have the bond.

He looked down, and grinned at me, feral.

"Damn straight, I'm yours."

And then he pumped once, twice, and came.

He filled me as I shook. I looked down at the black flame on his chest and knew that I might be embarrassed later, because that wasn't going away.

That wouldn't fade like the mark on my body would. No, I had marked him body and soul, and now the world would know.

After we cleaned each other up, he kissed me softly.

"I'll wear your mark with pride."

I blushed. "I didn't really mean to do that."

He frowned and I shook my head. "I didn't mean to maim you."

He took my hand, put it above the mark on his chest.

"I'm damned pleased about the mark. It's not just a

bite, it's more. And it's all mine. Unique. I'll fucking take it."

I cupped his face and swallowed hard.

He cupped my face, looked into my eyes, and growled low. "I know that you're afraid. And so am I. But we're going to fix this. I'm tired of things pushing us apart and hurting our Pack. Of hurting us. So we're going to fight. Because I'm not letting you go, Dara. We're going to find a way."

"I trust you."

And I did. I just didn't trust fate.

Because I was so damn afraid of what the cost would be to have each other. And what the cost would be to keep our Pack safe. We had been far too lucky, even with the scars on our souls.

And that told me that we wouldn't be lucky for long. My gift was death, and I had saved Cruz once before. I didn't think the fates would allow me to do it again. But I refused to lose him.

So perhaps the only way to stop that, was to lose myself.

*

LATER, WE STOOD WITH THE WITCHES OF OUR territory, ready to create what should have been repaired years ago, until those in power had taken over.

Had taken everything.

They betrayed their own kind, so now we had to fix it.

We were righting a wrong, although it wasn't the wrong I had been thinking of before.

"We're all here," Jade said into the silence.

Hannah, the earth witch and co-Healer of the Redwood Pack, came forward. She was beautiful, her skin glowing. She looked to be my age, though I knew she was much older. Having mated with not one but two members of the Redwood Pack led her to have an extended life, much like many of the Pack members here.

She always smelled of home and warmth. I was friends with her children, and though Hannah hadn't been able to help me control my powers, she always tried when the coven hadn't. They had kicked her out just like they had kicked me out.

"I do believe you should be the one to start us."

I blinked. "Me? But you're *Hannah*. The Healer." I put so much emphasis on the word that people laughed around me.

I looked at my friends who had been part of the Packs for years, and shook my head.

"Seriously, Leah, she's Hannah. She should be the leader of the coven."

Leah, a Talon Pack member and water witch just shook her head. "We all voted when you were not here. Sorry."

"She's not really sorry," Dhani added. Dhani was a Talon Pack member as well, and a spirit witch. She had helped create the coven along with Leah, and had been thrown to the curb when someone else had come in and cleaned house.

Nico and Gina, both next generation witches—as they called themselves—just shook their heads. They were shifter and witch, something that was new to the Packs as more witches and humans mated with shifters.

"Sorry. You're bringing the new talent in, you're going to have to deal with all of us," Nico said.

I looked at all of them. At my friends old and new, and just sighed.

"We're here to create a safe haven of growth and strength."

"And that, my dear, just that one sentence right there, is why we need you." Jade smiled softly, her eyes dancing with laughter.

"You brought us here, child, now lead us."

I looked at Leta, who smiled as Bishop put his hand around her shoulders and held her close.

We witches weren't the only ones in the room, the Alphas of the Packs were around us, as were Cruz and the other Heirs. When I looked to Cruz, he came forward.

"Do you want privacy?" he asked.

I winced. "I think this needs to be just witches. I know the council will be made of witches, humans, and shifters, but I think when we create this, I think we need to be just us. Which sounds wrong."

"We have Pack meetings separate from alliance meetings, separate from council meetings—you are not wrong," Chase said. He leaned forward, past Cruz, and kissed the top of my head.

Cruz growled, low, possessive, and Chase grinned. "Called it. It's about damn time."

My heart broke, but Cruz didn't shake his head.

"It's not complete yet, but it will be."

Chase looked between us. "Later of course. And we'll talk."

He left, as did the other Pack members, the Alpha of the Central Pack kissing his mate Nico hard on the lips.

Nico blushed right to the tips of his ears, and I just shook my head.

"We aren't the only magic users in the area, but we are the ones that I know we can trust."

"We don't really know you," Gina said to the others. She was also the co-Enforcer of the Redwood Pack. Her job was to protect on so many levels, so I understood why she was cautious.

"You don't need to know us, you just need our powers, right?" Bishop growled. But I heard the fear in his tone.

"Why don't you like wolves, dearest?" Hannah asked softly.

Bishop flinched. "You want us all to come together and use our magics to protect, to find a way to aid others. To be all encompassing and loving, but we're all violent. We're all selfish. Somebody inside your former coven betrayed you. They killed the others and took control. And now they're dead, their magic siphoned. Someone took that magic and attacked us. They killed Iris, nearly killed Dara. And we're just supposed to be okay? To act as if none of that happened?"

I shook my head. "No, that's why we're here. All of us have had to deal with the former coven and its ilk pushing us away. Each of us has our own way of doing magic. We're not what they thought we should be. We were either too close to the wolves, or our magic wasn't perfect enough. It scared them or it was too powerful. But there are others like us. Others that don't even know their potential yet. We need to protect them. Just like we need to protect the Packs. The wards have always been a blend of witch and shifter. The moon goddess and our goddesses have always worked together, and yet we have failed each other. We can't do it again."

"Well said," Hannah muttered.

I smiled, even though my heart raced. "You've heard the prophecy, what the moon goddess said through me. I don't know who I need to bring back. You know I'm a death witch. I do not harvest souls, but I must protect who I can. I must right the wrongs that the goddess can't do herself. But in order to do that, I need to know that my Pack is safe. Somebody's out there trying to kill us, trying to wipe us from the world because they want our power, and they want to be the ones in charge. So we will fix this. We will stop them. But we need to do it together."

"And just hold hands and sing merry tunes?" Declan

asked. But I knew he was just being himself, fear obvious in his tone.

"If we fucking have to. Or maybe we can just be who we've needed to be this entire time but we don't have to hide it anymore. The vampires are using a witch. That magic user has stolen our friends' powers. They have siphoned them and now we need to stop it. We need to protect our people and the people who depend on us. There is a demon out there who is controlling all of this, and we aren't strong enough right now to stop him."

"We weren't strong enough to stop the first demon," Hannah said, an eon of history and pain in her tone. "It took sacrifice and death and other demons to stop him. It took the tears of our young and the blood of our souls and loved ones in order to stop that demon. And if there are more out there, creating these vampires, it's going to take more than what we have. It's going to take all of us."

I looked at all of them and nodded. "So yes, we will hold hands, and we will create a governing body that will not be there to tell people what to do or what not to do, but to be a touchstone. We need a way to put our knowledge together, our powers together."

"Then let's get to it," Nico said, as he snapped his fingers. "Because I don't know about you, but my magic's sparking right now, and we need to get it done."

And one by one we each nodded.

There would be rules and regulations later. There

would be ways to understand what this coven meant and what it needed to do later. But this was the first step.

I held out my hands, and Jade took one, and Hannah the other, and as each person gripped the next person's hands, magic pulsed.

No words were needed, because with each connection we forged who the coven would be. It was not something broken, not something turned into darkness. It wasn't what the coven had turned into.

No, this was hope. And hope wasn't something I had ever had. Not until Cruz.

I closed my eyes, and I let the magic flow.

"We are the coven. We are the magic users. Through fire and earth and air and water and spirit, through metal and blood and darkness and death. Through who we are through soul and might, we are the coven. And we will protect, we will fight, and we will be. I vow to use my magic to protect, to show the world that we have a right to be here. And I vow to you, my coven members, to be who you need me to be."

I hadn't meant to say the words, but as each person made the same vow, I knew we had set in stone a marker. A way for us to begin.

As the magic dissipated, it wrapped me in a new promise. I opened my eyes and smiled at my friends.

And then the walls shook, someone screamed, and an explosion rocked the room.

CHAPTER SEVENTEEN

Cruz

The explosion knocked the wolf at my left to the ground, but he rolled quickly to his feet, and moved at his Alpha's command.

We were in the council area, the neutral place between the four Packs. We didn't have the full arsenal of our Packs, but whoever was attacking us didn't care about that.

Or perhaps they did, and they were coming after the witches, knowing that we shifters didn't have our entire arsenal with us.

"Go!" Cole ordered his wolves near him, and I knew

the Alpha of the Central Pack was feeling the same thing I was.

Our mates were in that building, the building currently falling down around itself.

I ran towards the front door. This place had been rebuilt countless times, as if it were a symbol of what others needed to destroy in battle.

I didn't care about that symbol or the fact that no matter what we did, people kept trying to kill us. All that mattered was I needed to get to my mate.

The door slammed open and Jade stood there, her hair billowing around her face, a wicked grin lashing out at anyone who dared growl at her.

"Well, I guess it's time to party."

She snapped her fingers, and a ball of fire appeared in her hand.

"Duck, wolf. You're going to want to duck."

Considering she was looking directly at me, I did as she said.

The fireball flew over my head, and I turned to see the mindless vampire behind me burst into flames.

"That's something you don't see every day," Steele said with a harsh laugh.

"You're seriously going to have to teach me that," Gina, the Redwood Pack Enforcer and fellow fire witch said, as she moved towards her Alpha, and everybody began to fight as one.

I moved through the masses, pinning down a vampire as it came at me.

These weren't just vampires coming at us.

No, the human hate group was here too.

Someone was fucking organizing all these people—who was it?

It had to be somebody that knew the workings of our Pack, or at least knew our Packs. Because they knew we'd be here. They knew we'd be at the council.

Dara slid out of the door then, Leta by her side. "We need to keep Leta safe. She's not a fighter."

I nodded, and then Hayes came forward.

"Ma'am," Hayes said, as he nodded.

The small older woman looked up at the big polar bear in human form and smiled. "Oh. I like you. You have such a kind soul." She went up to her tip toes and patted his cheek. "You fight, I'll protect you."

He raised a brow. "Ma'am?" he asked, as I pulled Dara to me.

"I might not be able to fight, but I can protect. I'm a blood witch. And vampires love their blood."

She winked, looking years younger, and then Hayes was off, Leta at his side.

I crushed Dara to me and kissed her hard on the mouth. "Are you okay?"

She looked unharmed, but I couldn't tell for sure. Because our bond wasn't whole. I fucking hated this.

"I'm fine. I promise. But there's something wrong.

That magic that I felt before in the alley? It's here. But I don't know who it is. Who is controlling these vampires?"

A very familiar laugh hit my ears, sending denial and shock down my spine. I pushed Dara behind me as I turned to see a familiar face.

The face of someone who shouldn't be here.

"You are dead," I blurted, as Lily stood there in ripped jeans, a red leather jacket, her eyes bright and manic.

"Oops."

"Oops? Lily. What are you doing here?" Dara asked as she moved past me. I tried to grip her, tried to pull her back, but in my confusion I was slow to react.

"Lily," she said, as things began to make sense, a disgusting and wicked sense that I did not want to think about.

"You never understood me. You always thought that I was this weak witch who would never become anything. You looked down on me. But you didn't realize that I had more power than you could ever hold."

She held out her hand and a jagged shard of vampire darkness mixed with what seemed to be crystal and glass.

That was the light magic that Dara must have felt before. It had to be.

"I don't understand," Dara said from beside me, and I echoed her thoughts.

"You will. But not yet."

And then Lily moved so quickly I couldn't even follow.

The earth rumbled beneath my feet, and I pulled Dara out of the way, part of the roof falling on where we had just stood.

"Oh my goddess. How could it be Lily?" she asked.

I cupped her face. "I don't know. Maybe Valac turned her and we didn't realize. Maybe something happened that we couldn't figure out. But we need to stop this. The humans and the vampires are working together here, trying to kill us. So let's protect our people, and then we'll figure out exactly what the fuck Lily was just doing."

Because Lily had been part of our inner council. She might have been almost human, or at least that's what we had thought, but she knew things. Had fought beside us.

And it seemed like she had fucking betrayed us.

She hadn't scented of vampire, she didn't have fangs. She wasn't one of the good vampires that Leta had mentioned.

No. This was something else.

I wanted to be sick.

"Go back to your hell, wolf," a man said from beside us as he took his gun and began to spray bullets through the field.

Skye went down, holding her arm as she cursed, before she scrambled back up, and Chase roared above her.

The human's eyes widened as he realized exactly what he was surrounded by. Yes, he had a weapon, but the monsters from his nightmares were around him, and he wasn't going to be able to stop them all.

"Are you okay?" Chase asked, and Skye nodded, rolling her shoulders. "I'm fine. I don't need Hayes."

"You fucking do need Hayes," he snapped, as the big polar bear and Leta came forward.

But before Hayes could move, Leta put her hand over Skye's arm and smiled.

"This won't hurt. I promise."

The blood witch whispered under her breath, her magic warm against my skin as I fought vampires, taking one down after another, and she healed the Alpha's mate.

I had never seen any magic like it. Blood pooled around her arm, not just Skye's but her own, and the blood witch healed the injury.

"I told you, a blood witch isn't evil. We're just different." The older woman winked, once again looking like she had a new energy of her, and Hayes grinned.

"Well, you're a surprise."

Wynter came forward, blades in hand.

"Okay, I'm standing by you," she said, looking between the big polar bear and the blood witch. "Seriously. They're coming over the west ridge. I know more of our team is on the way, but there are a lot more vampires and humans than we thought."

I cursed, and went back to the fight.

Audrey was on her headset, directing people to where they needed to be. This could just be a distraction for another attack, but I didn't think so. Not with Lily here.

Lily. I still couldn't believe it.

"Where do you want us?" I asked, Dara at my side. I wasn't going to let her leave me, not when I knew that she had to be exhausted from keeping the wards up for as long as she had.

"Over to the east. Nico is over there with Cole, but Adalyn's back at the den."

I nodded, knowing that Adalyn would want to be here, but the Alpha's mate of the Centrals was heavily pregnant, and she wouldn't want to risk fighting out here with the rest of us.

"Stand back for a moment," Dara said into the din of fighting, and I nodded, showing my fangs as a vampire came too close.

Dara pressed her palms together, chanted under her breath, and moved her hands forward, palms outstretched as she pushed dark smoke from between her hands.

Eyes widening, I looked at her, her skin radiating a glow that I hadn't sensed before.

That little tethered strip between us, that one that was soul-to-soul because of her harvester death witch powers, throbbed.

"What was that?

"My power. Now that I'm connected to the coven, I can breathe again. I know it's not totally fixed, but it's close. We can do this. We have to do this."

"Yes, we will."

I looked towards the battlefield as Cassius fought, taking down vampire after vampire, his mate Novah at his side. Hayes, Leta, and Wynter moved as a unit to help the Healer with the injured and pick up anyone who needed a burst of energy. With Leta helping Hayes like she was, Wren could tend to the more seriously injured. Wynter used her skills as a fighter to keep them safe, even though I knew the large polar bear could use one paw to take them down in an instant. Wren moved quickly between them all, taking care of those that the Omega and others couldn't. Sawyer was out there, fighting with a grace that I hadn't realized the human had.

Steele ordered people around, keeping the wolves on task, as Jade fought using her power, spurts of fire blending with Declan's metal in a magical array that I had never seen before in my life, and didn't know if I ever would again.

Wolves, humans, and witches from all of the Packs fought as a unit, using the skills we'd trained for, yet with the number of vampires increasing with each passing moment, I was worried we wouldn't be enough.

But we were stronger than we had been before, and now Lily and the others would realize it.

Bishop stood in the back, hands outstretched as he whispered words to Audrey, speaking coordinates and numbers as if he could sense exactly who came on our land and where. Perhaps as a mental mage he was able to figure out where the vampires and humans were coming from so we could stop them.

I wasn't sure, as we had never fought like this before. It wasn't just fang against fang, claw against claw. It was a whole new battle, and it didn't make any sense to me, but it seemed to be working.

The humans who had come with hate in their eyes worried me. They only came at the Packs, but they had fear in their eyes when it came to the vampires at their side. It didn't make any sense. If they hated anything not human, why were they working with them?

Someone was telling lies, and it wasn't us.

"*Lily*," Dara growled.

The woman that used to be our friend, our Packmate, smiled at us.

"Hello, Dara darling. I'm surprised to see you walking after that alley. But then again, you always bounce back, no matter how many times I added those different poisons to your herbs, you never fell. The wards never fell, and I wonder why that was, because you aren't the strong witch you think you are. You are death. You literally hold death in your hand, and you never became the power you could be."

"You tried to kill my mate?" I growled, as Dara stilled beside me.

"Your mate? A death witch can't mate. She doesn't even have a soul to make it happen. She borrows souls. She's a leech. She's not good enough to be a mate. You should have stayed dead, Cruz, and then none of this would have happened. Instead, my consort had to go to extraordinary measures to ensure that I'm safe. Because he loves me. Your little death witch could never love you."

"You were the one that kept sabotaging everything that we did. We should have been able to stop the shards of dark magic long before we had. You sabotaged us."

"My consort needed me. I did as I was told because I am a good mate. And you can't even create a bond. You are nothing. You're an abomination."

"You leech power!" Dara screamed.

"You take, you don't give. Don't you fucking talk about my mate like that," I growled. "And who the hell is your consort?

"Don't you know?" Lily asked with a smile.

"Tell us," I said, but I knew the answer. We all did.

"Malphas is mine. He is the true ruler of us all. And soon he will bathe in your blood and your power and you will realize exactly who should have controlled us all. You run around in your little Packs and play in your little gardens and you pretend that you're fighting within yourselves or trying to govern one another. But you are nothing. You don't know the true power. He created the vampires. He created all of this. And you can't even create a mating bond."

"You? You did all this?" the human beside her said. "You begged us for help. You told me where these monsters would be. That you were hurt by them. And yet here you are, *with* them. You bitch! You're one of them. A monster. An abomination. You lied to all of us and you will burn in the hell fires for your treachery. You let good people, good *humans*, die because you're a fucking liar and bitch. A monster!"

I didn't recognize him, but from the look of absolute horror on his face, I had a feeling that Lily had promised things that she had no plan to follow through on to get this human to fight.

Lily rolled her eyes, and I hardly recognized her. This wasn't the sweet human who joined the Pack as a child. We protected her from Blade, had kept her safe. But something else had taken her. She was consort to Malphas.

And I did not even recognize her.

"Matthew. Humans Only Group? Your initials are HOG. Of course, I'm going to use you. You are a means to an end. And soon you will bow before your masters. Or at least your people will. Because I am done hiding. I'm done pretending to be the sweet little bit of a Lily that gets nothing done. I am the consort of a demon. Of our master. And you will bow before me just as you will to him."

"You whore!" Matthew called out as he raised his gun.

Lily grinned before reaching out, that jagged light magic slamming into Matthew's chest. I moved forward, trying to help, to do something, but the magic at Lily's command mixed with Dara's magic—which was keeping our people safe—held us back. The human let out a shocked gasp, then looked down at the hole in his chest, as if unbelieving of what he saw.

I wanted to move, wanted to help. Just because this Matthew and his hate group had come after us, didn't mean that he needed to die in that way. Nobody deserved to die like that.

As Matthew fell, Lily sighed.

"What *are* you?" Dara asked, echoing my thoughts.

Lily sent out a wave of magic, and Dara matched the motion, light meeting darkness, and yet this light wasn't good. This light was a blend of all the magic that she had siphoned and stolen from those she killed.

As people raged around us, fighting to protect the innocent, fighting to protect each other, I looked towards my mate, wide-eyed.

"How can I help?" I called out, my wolf shaking, needing to get out.

"I don't know. I don't know why she did this. But if we don't stop her, she's going to hurt us all. She could take all of our magic. I don't know how the demon created vampires. And we have to figure that out too. There has to be a way for us to use that knowledge for good. But there's something else, there has to be. Lily has done something. And I'm afraid of what that means."

The humans were fleeing, their leader dead, confusion evident—we would deal with them later. But first, we had to beat the vampires. Lily had brought with her the horde. The ones that were newly made that couldn't fight for themselves, and just fought in a frenzy of death and horror.

We had to save our people. I kept fighting, kept taking down one vampire after another. I beheaded one, stabbed another through the heart. But they kept coming.

How many humans had Lily and Malphas sacrificed in order to create them? How close were we to the end because of this monster's madness?

"We need to get out of here. We need to regroup," I growled.

Dara nodded. "We have to. I don't know what to do."

"I'll get you out of here. I promise you."

I turned, slamming my fist into the nearest vampire, as Lily sent a shockwave of magic directly towards Dara. I moved without thinking, knowing there was only one thing I could do.

I slammed Dara to the ground, covering her with my body, as hot, molten magic sliced into my back, through my chest, and radiated through my body. My eyes widened, my mouth opened, and I looked at Dara's screaming face until there was nothing.

CHAPTER EIGHTEEN

Dara

The bond between Cruz and I snapped. It wasn't darkness, it wasn't death, it couldn't be. Whatever connected to me as a harvester witch tugged at Cruz, and I refused to let go.

Everybody scrambled around me, kind of shouting orders, but I couldn't pay close attention. Hayes and Jade were above me, pulling Cruz off as they tried to heal him, but I knew they couldn't.

No, it would have to be me. I stood up, pushed Steele's hands away as he tried to grip my shoulders, and I staggered, looking around as my own magic shook within my hands.

"Where is she?" I screamed. "Where is she!"

"She's gone," Steele snapped, the anger in his voice so strong that I could feel it along the bonds that connected me as Pack.

I wasn't a wolf. I wasn't a shifter. But I was a witch. I was coven, and I was Pack, and I could feel every single person on our side on this battlefield.

The building where we had created the new coven, where we had created the council, was demolished. They hurt so many, and I would think about that soon.

But first, I needed to scream.

"Why did you let her go?" I asked, refusing to look behind me. I refused to look at what would be there. And who would be there. I didn't want to see who was on the ground behind me. Because I could hear people shouting and crying and trying to save him.

But they wouldn't. They wouldn't be able to save the man that I loved. Because Lily had done this. She had done this, and I would find a way to make her pay.

Chase cupped my face and forced me to look at him.

"Lily. Lily did this, and I want to know why."

"She's the demon's. He got her. I don't know how, but he got her, and she tried to kill me. She tried to kill all of us. I don't know how to fix this. I need to fix him."

"Breathe. Breathe."

Skye was talking to me, telling me something, but I wasn't listening.

I turned away.

People were slowly getting up from the battlefield, and I could sense death.

What had called to me as the witch of darkness finally breathed into life. She sang into a world that had never been allowed to be hers before.

Jade was in front of me then, her eyes wide. "What do you need us to do? What do you need us to do?"

She said the words slowly, as if she were trying to pull me out of my own magic, and she was.

Because Jade knew me. Just like I knew her. We had hidden aspects of our magic, we all did, and yet I couldn't hide mine anymore.

"I need the coven, I can do this. The prophecy said I can do this, and I will."

Chase was there. "My brother is dead, I can't feel him along the bonds. Dead." His voice broke as he said the words.

"I'll fix him, Alpha. I'll fix it. I did it before, and I'll do it again."

Lightning crashed above us as it began to rain, the drops slamming into us, as if they were shards of pain and agony and memory.

Jade snarled, but the flames on her hands continued to burn, as if the water itself refused to douse her flame.

"Leah, can you use your water talents to repel the rain?" she asked.

The water witch came forward. "I can, if you need me."

"No, I need her powers for this. Create the circle, the wolves too. Anyone with a bond to him. Protect the wounded, whoever needs to fight, keep fighting. But whoever is able and has the power, help me."

"Anything you need," Chase whispered. "Save my brother."

He kept saying *brother*. Because he had accepted Cruz as his without thought. Because they had always been brothers. They had always been blood.

The others circled me, metal and magic and fire and blood and earth and water and spirit. Everything that we had been told we had to hide from even other magic users. We were not the old coven that would shame and push down anyone different than us. We were everyone, power in our own right. Wynter stood there, hand clasped with Sawyer's as the two humans watched, and I knew they would give anything to protect each other. To protect all of us. Because there was power in humanity, in the giving of self, and they understood it, but Lily hadn't. Lily had always tried to get more power, and it was never enough.

We were all our own power, and Lily hadn't seen that. She craved more, not acceptance, but power itself. And within me I held the power of what I could be, but I had suppressed it. I had hidden who I was because I was scared of it, but I wouldn't be scared any longer.

Because I finally looked down. I finally let myself see.

Cruz lay below me, eyes wide and unseeing in death.

My heart threatened to burst, but I ignored it. I

couldn't breathe. I wanted to break, but I couldn't. I couldn't feel anything. If I did, I'd know that this could be the end. That there was no coming back.

He was gone. He sacrificed himself for me, because Lily had used her stolen and twisted magic to try to kill me, and yet Cruz had stepped in front of me.

The humans tried to kill us, had tried to take what they thought was abomination and push us back. But they hadn't even realized, it seemed, that they had been fighting with their enemy. I didn't know what would come with that, and soon we would have to deal with it, but at the moment all that mattered was Cruz.

I knelt and put my hand over his chest. I couldn't feel his heartbeat, there was nothing there, but I could still feel the bond. Not the mating bond, because the goddess hadn't given us that, but she had given us something else. And I would fight for it. I would crawl for it. I would beg for it.

"Goddess, I call upon you. I am the true harvester death witch. I am death and life and power. I call forth the power of the coven and our Pack and our people, and I am telling you, I will go back. I will do what is right, and I will go back."

Jade began to chant a spell unheard of in these times, and I didn't know how she knew it, but I had a feeling the goddess herself was speaking through Jade. The others repeated the words, bloody and bruised and broken, but no one else had died. The only person dead on the field was my mate, and I would not allow this to be permanent.

I held death in my hand, and I refused to let anybody else take him from me.

I closed my eyes, and I leapt.

On the physical plane I might still be kneeling by Cruz, my hand on his chest as my friends and family and strangers who didn't even know us circled and protected us. I hadn't let myself feel until this moment. I had stood looking at the abyss before I had even fallen into where I now flew.

I wouldn't let him die. He couldn't. Everything hurt, and I wanted to scream and fight and claw, but there was nothing I could do except this.

My physical body would be there, and the others would keep me safe, they would protect each other like they always did, but for now I needed to be here for Cruz. Because he waited.

I fell, the wind billowing around my hair and my dress. I knew I would fall, and it would hurt, and I would smash into a thousand pieces, and it would be worth it. It had to be.

When the earth came and the impact shattered me, I let it. A thousand pinpricks of sensation, of agony and torment, slammed into me, and then I was human. I was whole, and I stood as the world screamed. Lava flowed from a far-off mountain, and the jagged edges of rocks and magma created spindly fingers that reached out to try to grab me. But it was all an illusion.

This was death, and yet it wasn't. This was the between, the moment betwixt.

I was the harvester of death, and this was mine, and I knew who I was here to find.

Cruz stood there, waiting, in his wolf form, that silver pelt of his glorious under the dark moon. He looked at me, his eyes full of knowing. He was here. This was his soul.

I moved towards him, but the darkness came, a shadowed spindly and slender figure until it looked at me with Lily's eyes.

"You fought against the wrong witch. I will return to my body, and I will kill you. I will make you pay for all that you have done. You have hurt so many of us, I will make you pay."

The darkness that was Lily's shadow, the person that she had once been before she gave into the cravings, smiled at me. "You will realize that I'm not who you think I am. Or perhaps you already have. You sacrificed so much, and yet what comes to you? Nothing."

She put her hand out, that black smoke of death—true death—coming towards me. I held up my hands, the ball of golden light that was my soul, and Cole's, and Cruz's, and everyone's that I had ever touched, lighting up the dark crevice as if it had been plunged into the sun itself.

"You will never come for us. I will always beat you. I am far more powerful than you could ever realize." And then Cruz was there, shifting in one swift moment from wolf to human. He was clothed in the same clothes he wore on the battlefield.

"If you touch my mate, I'll gut you. I am the brother of the Alpha, the Heir of the Aspen Pack. You might have hurt my body, but you will never take my soul. You are nothing."

He gripped my free hand, the magic growing between us, and I smiled.

I was the true harvester death witch, and I controlled death and life, and nobody would ever be able to touch that, except Cruz. Because Cruz held my soul.

And as Lily smiled, the figment of her imagination fading into the distance, it happened.

Just like that, wind slammed into us, like we were in the middle of a tornado, I turned to my mate.

And the mating bond slid into place.

It wasn't a normal one, it couldn't be. For I had already created not one but two bonds of death and life between us.

I would save him, as he would save me, just like we had always been meant to. But as the mating bond snapped into being, it encased the threads of our deaths.

We were our own fate, and we were stronger for it.

I cupped his face and put my hand over his chest. Again, there was no heartbeat. For he was not alive, nor was he dead. He was in between, and I would save him.

"I need to take you back, but it's going to hurt. It's

going to feel like we are both being stabbed over and over with a thousand icy shards of pain, but I will bring you back."

"You better not fucking stay behind," he growled.

I swallowed hard, tears filling my eyes. "I love you. I'm not going to let myself stay. I'm going to fight. Because I've just mated you. And I'm going to protect our people."

"I love you, too. I've loved you for far longer than I've cared to admit." And then he kissed me, and it was real. This was real. This was our souls combining in a way that no one else could ever touch.

He pulled back and he pressed his forehead to mine. "Am I going to remember this? I didn't remember the last time."

I smiled. "You will. I'm going to make sure of it." I turned, looking beyond us, as I knew that he wasn't the only reason I had come. Cruz had died for a reason, one that I didn't want to think about. But the prophecy was true, and this wasn't the wrong I was righting.

No, this wrong had been waiting for us for years. And I would fix it.

"Will they remember?" Cruz asked.

"I won't let them. They can't."

"You're going to have to fight. I'll pull them, but you're going to have to pull all of us. You're going to have to be stronger than you have ever been.

"For you? Of course I will."

I turned and held up my hands.

"If you want to come back. If you want to be where you should have been all this time, I will take you. You shouldn't have died on that battlefield. I'll fix this. This is my promise to you."

And then Tatiana of the Thames Pack slid her hand into mine, her young and innocent face relaxed in trust. I didn't know what she had been through, what could have occurred in this plane of existence, but this wasn't her death, and I would fix it.

And Blake Jamenson of the Redwood Pack, my Alpha's cousin, and the man who never should have left us, looked at me and at my outstretched hand. "Will it hurt you? I don't want it to hurt you."

Tears filled my eyes and I swallowed hard. "No," I lied. "I'll bring you back. I promise. They miss you. Your family misses you."

Blake put his hand in mine and power rocked through me, stabbing me over and over again. I looked up into the sky, the darkening clouds telling me that the storm that raged above us here and on the physical plane was not natural.

"Just hold me, Cruz."

He did, and I shot up towards the sky, pulling three souls in my wake. Agony spread through me as Cruz screamed, and I looked over my shoulder at him. Long claws raked over his body, the demons not of that plane but of darkness sliced through him, over and over again. The others screamed as well, but I kept moving. Cruz would remember this. He would want to. But I wouldn't let the others so I protected them, taking the pain just as Cruz did, as they stabbed and they clawed and they tried to bring them back to death, but I wouldn't allow it.

And as I screamed again, I opened my eyes, and there was silence.

Cruz lay below me, his eyes open and filling with tears. I let out a shocked gasp, trying to breathe as he cupped my face and the mating bond warmed.

"I love you," he whispered.

And then someone screamed, a shocked cry.

"Blake?" Skye asked, her voice cracking.

"Tatiana?" another person asked.

It had been years since they died, their bodies burned to ash, but they were back. *I had brought them back.* I had done magics that I shouldn't have, magics that would scar, but this was the goddess's choice. I knew it. She had given me this power, this prophecy, and I would use it.

I had righted a wrong of the innocent. I brought back those who never should have left us.

Blake and Tatiana would have a second chance at life. A second chance from their death.

And my Cruz would have his third, and I would have my extended life with him.

For I was the power. I was life and death, just like all of us in this field.

People spoke to me, but I couldn't hear them. I looked

between the three I brought back, then down at my mate as he sat up, unharmed, and holding my face.

My mate was alive. And that was the only thing that mattered in this moment.

It was the only thing that could.

CHAPTER NINETEEN

Cruz

I PACED THE LIVING ROOM, GOING FROM ONE CORNER to the next, while everyone spoke around me at once, trying to come to terms with what had just happened.

I didn't think I'd ever come to terms with it.

I remembered. The pain, the screaming, the absolute darkness that wasn't dark.

But she had brought me back. She had come for me, because no matter what, we would always protect each other.

"Lily. It was Lily?" Wren asked, her eyes wide. She wasn't crying, I didn't think the submissive lynx Healer could cry right then. She just sat on the couch, eyes wide, her hands together.

After we had come back from wherever the hell we had been, everything had happened quickly. The Redwoods and Talons took Tatiana and Blake back. Every single Healer, including Wren, had looked them over, and no one had explanations.

I didn't think there could be.

Their bodies were exactly how they had been nearly five years ago when they died.

They hadn't aged, at least not physically. Dara explained that neither one of them would remember what had happened during the timeframe. And from what I remembered from that hellscape, I didn't think they wanted to know.

In both instances of my seemingly dying, I had been gone for moments, maybe minutes at most. The others had been gone for years.

They didn't need to remember that hell. If it was hell. Dara had called it an in-between, a betwixt, and maybe that was it.

I would want to speak with Blake and Tatiana soon. We would need to. I needed to. My wolf did as well.

Dara would, though I didn't know how that would go. They had made their choice, but hell, would they even remember making it?

The ramifications of everything that had just

happened were so out of this sphere, that none of us knew what to do about it.

"She lied to us. All of us," Wynter spat. All of us were there, at least as many could fit inside Chase and Skye's large home.

But it felt as if I was standing on that same abyss, wondering how the hell we ended up here.

"She's gone. She faked her death?" Audrey asked, her lioness in her eyes. "We gave her everything that we had. Her family was Pack, and when they died, we protected her. We raised her."

Her eyes widened and she looked at her mate.

Gavin winced. "You don't think that she hurt her parents, do you? You said she was five when they died. Of an illness."

"They were witches, both of them, who had become Pack because they wanted protection." Chase ran his hand over his face. "And we never figured out what that illness was. Dad was in charge then," he growled, and I looked at my brother. My *brother*, and I felt a sense of foreboding.

"I don't think she did it, but I don't think anything with Lily was accidental. Not with how this is turning out."

"So, either they died because they were witches and the coven didn't want them to have their power, Blade did it because he wanted power of his own—which is probably what happened—" Chase continued.

"Or you have another traitor," Sawyer cut in.

I looked towards the human, and almost wondered why he was there, but Jade was there.

Sawyer had bled for this Pack, for this coven. He deserved to be there, just like all of us did.

"Or that. But I don't know. We might never know unless we ask Lily, and I have a feeling that Lily is gone beyond what we know," Dara said into the quiet. I turned and held out my arm as she walked into the room. She slid next to me, and we leaned against the wall as we tried to come to terms with what happened.

"We're all here because we're trying to figure out what to do next," my Alpha began.

"Thank you for not kicking us out," Declan said casually, and I looked over to Bishop who sat quietly next to him. Sweat beaded on his temples and I could scent his fear. Every single shifter in here could. It was a putrid stench, but Bishop was trying to hide it, and we weren't going to point it out. It hurt my wolf, and I wanted to make him feel better, but I didn't think we could. We could just show him that not all of us were monsters. He had protected us, had worked beside Audrey to keep people in line and make sure we knew what was coming. He had sacrificed his own safety in order to help us, and that would not be forgotten. I just hated the idea that he was in pain. We all did.

"So what do we do next?" Dara asked. "Do we look for Lily? Malphas?"

"I would like to know who Malphas is," Jade added. "A demon. A real demon?"

"The Redwoods dealt with demons before I was born," Skye said. "My grandparents died because of a demon. I'm named after my grandmother. She sacrificed herself to protect my father, and a demon killed them. So yes, demons are real. That one was named Caym. He's gone, back to that hell dimension. But there are others. Others that took him away, and they came back. They created these vampires. I don't know if they're the exact same demons, but we'll find out. We'll find out who Lily's consort is, and we'll find out how to stop him."

"We'll do it because we don't have any other choice," I put into the silence. "We are Aspen, and coven. And friends," I added as I looked at Sawyer. The human's lips twitched into a small smile. "We have lost much, but we have gained even more as we fought side by side. We aren't the Aspens of the past, and there have been far more secrets than we'd even realized, but we're stronger now. Our wards are stronger, thanks to the people in this room, and the alliance surrounding us. I know that the unknown is scary as hell, but we will make plans with what we know."

Gavin cleared his throat. "I have Lily's new scent. It's different than it was. That siphoned magic? It's corrupted her, but we can track it."

Audrey looked pained, but nodded.

"We'll set up a team, and now that we know Lily is the one making these plans, we'll at least have a place to start."

"And what about HOG?" Steele asked, and nobody laughed. Because the Humans Only Group might have a hilarious name, but their actions hadn't been funny.

"We'll keep an eye on them," Chase answered. "I've already talked with the other Alphas and we're going to discuss what we can do with the human government. Humans don't get to kill us because they're afraid of us."

"I guess this means more PR?" Audrey asked, only a little sarcasm in her voice.

"I don't know what it means. But we're going to find out. We think Lily took Valac's place, at least based on what she said on the field. So that's an enemy with a face. One we can fight, even if it breaks us."

Dara sighed as she leaned into me.

"Her magic's different, corrupt."

Jade spoke next. "Then we stop her. I don't know Lily, so I don't have the same emotional attachment to her. But there are more magic users out there who have been hiding from covens who don't want them to have their power. So we find them, just like you did us, Dara. And we stop Lily. Because I might not be Pack, but I'm coven now. So I'll protect my people and those people who are allied with us. And those who don't want our help but need it. I'm tired of hiding in the shadows with my flame. And I know you, my dearest Dara, are tired of hiding what you are. And you didn't hide on that field."

I smiled. "No, you didn't. You were beautiful."

She blushed as somebody whistled under their breath, breaking the tension.

"Stop it."

"You saved us, Dara. My mate."

"You saved us too. Without you, I wouldn't have had the power to push Lily back."

"And you brought us back. We're a team. Remember that."

She grumbled something under her breath, and I kissed her fiercely on the mouth.

When someone else whistled and clapped, Chase cleared his throat.

"I suppose we have another mating ceremony to plan."

"It's about time," Steele grumbled.

"We will, soon," I whispered against my mate's lips.

I looked around at my family, at those of blood and bond and more. "We'll find this demon and we'll stop him. We'll find a way, just like we always have."

"We've shored up the wards, and our alliance is stronger because of the magic that we share between all of us," Dara added.

"There're also the other vampires," Leta put in, her voice soft. "They're out there, waiting for a friend, or at least for someone to acknowledge their existence. So let's find them, be an ally."

I turned to my Alpha who nodded tightly, and it was one more step. We were forming our allies, closing ranks.

Our enemy had a face and a name. We were the Aspens—we had fought death before and won. And we would do it again. But this time, I would have my mate by my side.

And nothing could stop us.

CHAPTER TWENTY

Dara

MY BODY HUMMED AS CRUZ'S HAND SLID UP MY SIDE, and I nearly let out a shaky breath, but did my best to hold it in.

It was so odd, this feeling that would never go away. Because this was it.

The bond was there. It was so different from what we had before. I had called that tether between us a bond, but in the end it was only a simple connection that could have been broken at any moment, even if I hadn't realized it.

This was a mating bond. What literal poems and sonnets were written about.

I could feel his love being sent along the mating bond,

and I sent mine right back, both of them colliding in a spark of passion as he kissed me, his hands continuing to roam.

"I have to meet with the others. We both have things to do."

I had a coven meeting, and he had a patrol meeting. We had responsibilities in our Pack. And now we had the strength to make things happen. This wasn't the end, but a beginning. Yet all I wanted to do was go down on my knees and take him into my mouth.

With a grin I started to do just that. I was on my knees, my hands on his belt buckle, when he groaned and pulled me away.

"You just said that you had a meeting. And while I would love my cock in your mouth, we need to stop."

I pouted up at him and cupped him through his jeans.

He groaned, rocking his hips. I don't think he realized that he was doing it.

And because I couldn't help myself, I undid his button, and slid down his zipper. His cock sprang forth and I cupped his balls, gripping him in my hand.

"You're already so hard. The tip already has a little come on it. I'm pretty sure I could take you down quite quickly, and no one would know."

"You are a menace," he growled, but then his hand was in my hair and my mouth was on his dick. I swallowed him whole, unable to stop myself. All I wanted to do was taste him. We had made love in the shower that morning, and then again trying to get dressed, as I bent over the dresser, naked, except for my bra. He had pounded into me from behind and tore my bra into pieces. He loved to watch my breasts bounce as he fucked me, and we watched each other through the mirror, pressing into one another with such frenzy, I knew it was beyond the mating frenzy, that mating heat. This urge was not just shifter, but it was magic, and it was everything.

I sucked him down, grateful for his endurance as a shifter. Even a witch would have trouble keeping up with me in this moment, but he was always hard for me, just like I was always wet for him. I swallowed him whole until he stiffened, ready to come. But he growled and pulled me up by my hair, that little sharp sting sending shocks right down to my wet pussy.

He pulled up my hips and slammed me to the wall. It should have been painful, but all I wanted was to have him inside me. Thankfully I was wearing a dress. It was easier to wear a dress when it came to him. He rucked my skirt up to my hips, pulled my panties to the side, and thrust into me in one movement. We both froze, groaning, as my body accommodated him. I was wet, so wet, and had nearly come with just one movement.

He grinned at me, his eyes wolf gold.

"Always fucking ready for me. My little hussy."

"My pussy is always wet for you, just like you're the charmer with a hard cock near me. You can't help it."

"I can feel you wanting me along the bond. I want you to come. Right now, on my cock, and then I'll fuck you."

I pouted. "And you're just going to stand there."

"I might do something, let's see." His gaze never broke from mine as he slid his hand between us and gently brushed his finger over my clit. A gentle brush, nothing too hard, nothing too soft, just a casual caress.

I shot off like a rocket, annoyed. I never came that easily. Usually it took forever, even thinking about Cruz, but no, he had put something along the mating bond, something that sent me right over, and as I screamed his name, my legs literally shaking around his hips, he pistoned into me, over and over again, until I was coming on the heels of that previous orgasm, and he was following me, filling me up as he growled into me. He bit my neck, just a soft bite, one that would leave a mark. My mating mark was still fresh enough for all to see, but he kept marking me. As if me looking like a chew toy would scare off everybody.

Maybe it would. It didn't matter. All that did matter was that Cruz was inside me, and I never wanted him to stop.

There was seriously something wrong with me. But I did not care. I just wanted him. After years of not being able to have him, he was mine.

"I love you," he whispered.

I wiped away tears as I kissed him.

"I love you, too. And now we're really going to be late."

"It's okay. We deserved it."

We cleaned each other up, and I was grateful that we kept a slight distance because if we kept touching each other, it was going to end badly for everybody.

"You're beautiful."

"No, I'm not. I look like I've just been fucked."

"Like I said. Beautiful." He laid a quick kiss to my lips, and then handed me a cup of coffee.

"We're going to be late but that's fine."

"I know."

"What's on your agenda today?" he asked, sipping his coffee. He leaned against the kitchen counter, my kitchen counter, as if he had been doing this forever. And maybe he had. We both loved our homes, but mine had my workshop, so he moved right in, and we would expand if we needed to. He was mine. And I loved him. And he was my mate. We would have a mating ceremony soon. But for now, we were getting to know one another like this. Everything had moved so fast before. It didn't matter that it had taken years to get to this point. Actual execution had been abnormally quick, even for a fated mating. We were getting to know each other's quirks, our needs, our desires.

And I was falling more and more in love with him every day.

"We have a coven meeting, and a lot to do."

"Is everyone going to be there today?"

"That's the plan. Jade, Leta, Declan, Bishop, Leah,

Dhani, Nico, Hannah, and Gina. And whoever else wants to come. But those are the main members."

"It sounds like every magical person in this area."

"Wynter might come as well."

He frowned. "Really? I didn't know Wynter wanted to. She's been quiet recently."

"Wynter lost her job because of the Humans Only Group. So she has more time on her hands, and has always been my apprentice, even if she doesn't have magical abilities of her own. The coven protects witches, teaches them, maybe we can help those who help us. I don't know, but Wynter needs a path. The Pack is part of it, and so are we."

"You're a good woman, Dara." He kissed me softly, and I pressed him back.

"Stop kissing me, or we're going to miss both of our meetings."

"True." He paused for a minute and frowned into his coffee cup. "What about Diana and Amelia?"

I swallowed hard, my hand shaking as I set down my coffee cup.

"When we found the notes from the old coven, I didn't believe it. About what Lily had done. She had been orchestrating with the new coven for so long, and we didn't even know."

"Don't blame yourself."

"A little part of me will. I called her a friend, I trusted her, and I was wrong. Yes, she used horrible ways to trick us all, but we fell for it, and I hate that that stain will be on us."

"But you don't carry that alone."

"I won't. Not anymore. As for Diana and Amelia, their memories were erased by the demon, and they were moved to the East Coast. We know that. Killing them would've killed the magic that the demon and Lily needed. And while the Eastern coven brought their memories back, I don't think Diana or Amelia or Amelia's child will ever move back. And I don't blame them. But I'm just so happy that they're not dead. The coven killed so many, even their own, but two of the strongest women that we know, the kindest witches, are alive. And for that I'm grateful."

"Me too, mate. You're going to be working on wards today?"

"That and weapons and personal wards. We have a lot to do, plus we're training. Not just trying to protect against vampires, but we're training each other in our own magics, trying to make sure that we are on the right path and we're not leaving anyone behind. It's what we should have done in the past, and what we had done until the new coven and this demon ruined everything."

"We're going to find him, and Lily."

Pain slid through me, and I nodded tightly. "We will. We're going to find her and we're going to make sure she pays for what she did."

"What about Blake and Tatiana?"

I let out a breath, grateful my coffee was gone because I didn't think I could take anything else in.

"They're not okay. I don't think they will be okay. Not for a while. But Tatiana's gone back with Allister, and her Pack will protect her. And we'll be here if they need us. And Blake? The Redwoods are strong. They're a good family. He'll find a way."

"They don't remember the years that they were gone, do they? At least I hope to hell they don't."

"Do you remember?"

"You do, and that scares the hell out of me. I remember parts, but not everything. And from what Blake said, he doesn't."

I hoped that was the truth. Because they had been dead. Gone, their bodies turned to ash, but I had brought them back somehow. Somehow their bodies had been returned whole, maybe scarred, but not in a way that could be seen.

I didn't know what would happen, and I didn't know if I would ever use my true harvester powers again. I didn't want to. It was painful, and horrible, and it meant circumventing fate. Or perhaps it didn't. Because the goddess herself had spoken it into existence. We had righted that wrong. They hadn't been meant to die, and now we had fixed it.

I didn't want to do it again.

"Are you meeting with your soldiers?"

"Yes. I'm working alongside Steele, who's having a hell of a time right now."

"He and Jade really do not get along."

"He doesn't trust her. You do, so I do, but Steele's different."

"He's the Enforcer, he's never going to trust anyone completely. Maybe not even his mate."

Cruz winced, before he leaned down and kissed me.

"I love you. Let's get to work, and then we'll come home, and you'll teach me a few spells."

I rolled my eyes. "At this point I'm just trying to teach you how to cook with herbs. Spices are your friend."

"As is microwave popcorn."

I rolled my eyes and kissed him again.

I had lived in silence for most of my existence. I had harbored my truths, my death, but now I lived in light.

We would find Lily, we would make her pay. We would find this demon and we would end this war. We finally had a way to protect ourselves. This was the change we had been waiting for, but the cost of it had been high, and I did not want to risk that again.

I finally had my mate, my Cruz. My path. And as he held me, just for a quick hug, a quick good morning, I knew that this moment would last in my memories until the end of my days. Just like every moment with him would.

He was my mate, finally and forever. And I was his witch.

CHAPTER

TWENTY-ONE

Jade

I WASN'T USED TO THIS. I PROBABLY SHOULD HAVE been, but at this point, I didn't know if it made sense to become used to it. I wasn't a Pack person, or even a person who wanted to be part of something like this. But it wasn't like I could go back. I had agreed, so here I was. A coven leader, I wouldn't say I wasn't the team player, because I had to be. But here I was, in a place I never thought I would be.

Sawyer was off doing something, probably making friends and finding secrets. It was what he was good at. It didn't matter that he had a kind soul, was a good person, he always made sure that we were safe.

My chest hurt, and I knew I was still bruised, still healing from the final battle.

Battle. As if I knew what I was doing with that. But I wasn't. I couldn't be.

"What's wrong?"

I stiffened at the sound of that deep voice, the one that I didn't want to deal with. All we did was fight, he didn't like me. I didn't like him. But my body wanted him. Traitor. My magic wasn't sure what it wanted.

"What are you doing here, Steele? Don't you have some form of training to do? Or obstacle course to master?"

His lips twitched. "Do you think I'm some human general or drill sergeant?"

I looked him up and down, my body tensing. He was damn sexy, even though I couldn't stand him. "Well, you do wear the boots."

He looked down at said boots, his lips quirking into a smile. "Maybe. And yes, I actually do have an obstacle course for my soldiers and lieutenants. I'm the Enforcer. I protect my people. And that includes you."

I raised a brow. "I'm not your Pack member. I'm not yours, Steele."

"You sure about that?"

He practically purred the words. "Are you sure you're not a cat?"

He raised a single brow. That was too sexy. I hated him. "No. You're the one that's all pussy."

I laughed, I couldn't help it, and he just grinned.

"You did not say that."

"I did. Mostly because you've been glaring at me, and I wanted to say something that was so ridiculous that you would think I was ridiculous, and you would stop yelling at me for just existing."

"I don't yell."

"No, you get all cold and icy. Which is ironic considering you're a fire witch."

I held up my hand, fire dancing along my palm. "I know, right? That icy-bitch attitude really does well with this." I snapped my fingers, and the flame dissipated.

"Your control of your own magic is pretty cool though."

I looked at him. "I hate you, you know."

"You hate me because I pushed you out of the way of that firefight."

"It was a bullet, if it was fire I could have handled it."

"And it wasn't, so I saved your life. Get over it. You've saved mine most likely."

"I did. We all have. I still hate you."

"No, you don't, cupcake."

My brows winged up. "Oh no. We're not doing cupcakes."

"I like cupcakes. Sweet. Taste smooth on my tongue."

I rolled my eyes. "Really? You're going back to that?"

"But you blush so prettily. I *am* here for a reason though."

I shook my head. "And what is that?"

"If you need us, you let us know. I know you're rebuilding the coven. I know you have power on your own. But you're Dara's friend. And because she's mated to my best friend, that makes you family."

I stilled, wondering what that warm sensation was within me. It couldn't be from a nice gesture. It couldn't be happiness. No, I was bitter and crone-ish. That's who I was. At least that's what I kept saying.

"Thank you for your concern."

"No problem. You need us, you let me know. Do you know where you're staying for now?"

I nodded tightly. "Thank you. Your Alpha already offered the den, but I don't feel comfortable yet within it."

"And why is that?"

I wasn't going to tell him, even though of all people he should probably know. However, even though he was an Enforcer, there was something else. And I couldn't quite put my finger on it. Until I did, I would keep my thoughts to myself. At least when it came to Steele.

"I should be going."

"You're hiding something. And I'll figure it out."

"Keep trying, wolf boy. I'll be here when you sniff out anything you need."

"Was that an innuendo? Because I can. You know how us dogs greet each other."

I blushed, hating myself, before I flipped him off and

he laughed. He left me alone then, and I wrapped my arms around myself, annoyed with him. I was always annoyed with him.

"You two are going to either kill each other one day, or do each other. I'm not quite sure which though."

I laughed as I looked over at my friend, the woman who had saved me countless times, and had put me in the middle of this mess. Though that wasn't fair. I had done that to myself.

"Dara. You're looking well fucked."

Dara rolled her eyes. "Stop trying to get a rise out of me."

"I'm pretty sure you already did that with your mate."

"Ha ha. You're hilarious, babe. Look, it's a dick joke."

"I know, shocking."

"Stop trying to push me away. You're not that good at it."

"I'm decent at it."

Left unsaid was the fact that I had pushed her away before. It was for her own safety. For all of our sakes. I just hadn't realized that the Aspens weren't who I had thought they were. And that reminded me...

"Dara. You're coven. I am too. But I'm not Pack. Sawyer isn't Pack."

She stiffened, staring at me. "Okay. I know that. Though, you could be if you wanted to."

I shook my head before I lowered my voice. "You

know there's something wrong with the bonds in the Pack, Dara. You can feel it, can't you? I'm an outsider, and I can only feel it through the connection with the coven, but there's something wrong."

Dara nodded, her eyes narrowing. "You're right. I only missed it because I didn't have the energy to focus on it. I don't think the wolves can sense it at all, because I know these people. These shifters would do anything for their Pack. To protect each other."

"Lily was a traitor." Dara flinched, and I hated that I just put it out there. But I needed to. "I'm sorry you were hurt. I'm sorry that this Pack is bleeding because of that woman. You know I hate traitors, I hate how they dig in and they take what is closest to you. But you know that's not what you're feeling. Lily doesn't have bonds to us. Doesn't have bonds to you. So, what is wrong with the Pack that the shifters can't tell, but the coven can?" I paused.

"There's someone else."

"And someone we must fear. We must find out before it's too late."

I stared at her, and I knew the worst was to come. Because Lily had betrayed them all. But I had a feeling there was something far worse waiting.

And if we didn't find it soon, no coven, no Pack, no trust would be enough to stand against it.

Next in the Aspen Pack series?
Find out what happens to Steele and Jade in Marked in Flames!

Want to read a special BONUS EPILOGUE featuring Cruz and Dara? CLICK HERE!

A NOTE FROM CARRIE ANN

Thank you so much for reading **Harbored in Silence!**

This book was a whole new avenue for the Aspens and I had so much fun! I wanted to get out of the den a bit and see the world of Packs from the other side. A witch-filled road trip seemed like the perfect way to make that happen!

Dara and Cruz were connected far before I met them but the didn't realize it. I'm so happy with how they finally fell for one another.

As for Lily.

Yes. I know.

I always knew.

And for Blake and Tatiana? I needed to right a wrong and knew that one day I would find a way. Three years ago when I came up with this series, I knew this moment would happen. I just needed to wait for it.

Now...well now things get interesting.

Next up? Things get messy with Jade and Steele in Marked in Flames. A huge thing is about to happen. Something I've been waiting for. And it's about time we figure out exactly what these vampires want.

And what a demon has been doing all along.

The Aspen Pack Series:

Book 1: Etched in Honor

Book 2: Hunted in Darkness

Book 3: Mated in Chaos

Book 4: Harbored in Silence

Book 5: Marked in Flames

And if you're in the mood for a paranormal romance outside the world of the Aspens:

The Ravenwood Coven Series:

Book 1: Dawn Unearthed

Book 2: Dusk Unveiled

Book 3: Evernight Unleashed

Want to read a special BONUS EPILOGUE featuring Cruz and Dara? CLICK HERE!

If you want to make sure you know what's coming next from me, you can sign up for my newsletter at www. CarrieAnnRyan.com; follow me on twitter at

@CarrieAnnRyan, or like my Facebook page. I also have a Facebook Fan Club where we have trivia, chats, and other goodies. You guys are the reason I get to do what I do and I thank you.

Make sure you're signed up for my MAILING LIST so you can know when the next releases are available as well as find giveaways and FREE READS.

Happy Reading!

ALSO FROM CARRIE ANN RYAN

The Montgomery Ink Legacy Series:

Book 1: Bittersweet Promises

Book 2: At First Meet

Book 2.5: Happily Ever Never

Book 3: Longtime Crush

Book 4: Best Friend Temptation

Book 5: Last First Kiss

The Wilder Brothers Series:

Book 1: One Way Back to Me

Book 2: Always the One for Me

Book 3: The Path to You

Book 4: Coming Home for Us

Book 5: Stay Here With Me

Book 6: Finding the Road to Us

Book 7: A Wilder Wedding

The Aspen Pack Series:

Book 1: Etched in Honor

Book 2: Hunted in Darkness

Book 3: Mated in Chaos

Book 4: Harbored in Silence

Book 5: Marked in Flames

The Montgomery Ink: Fort Collins Series:

Book 1: Inked Persuasion

Book 2: Inked Obsession

Book 3: Inked Devotion

Book 3.5: Nothing But Ink

Book 4: Inked Craving

Book 5: Inked Temptation

The Montgomery Ink: Boulder Series:

Book 1: Wrapped in Ink

Book 2: Sated in Ink

Book 3: Embraced in Ink

Book 3: Moments in Ink

Book 4: Seduced in Ink

Book 4.5: Captured in Ink

Book 4.7: Inked Fantasy

Book 4.8: A Very Montgomery Christmas

Montgomery Ink: Colorado Springs

Book 1: Fallen Ink

Book 2: Restless Ink

Book 2.5: Ashes to Ink

Book 3: Jagged Ink

Book 3.5: Ink by Numbers

Montgomery Ink Denver:

Book 0.5: Ink Inspired

Book 0.6: Ink Reunited

Book 1: Delicate Ink

Book 1.5: Forever Ink

Book 2: Tempting Boundaries

Book 3: Harder than Words

Book 3.5: Finally Found You

Book 4: Written in Ink

Book 4.5: Hidden Ink

Book 5: Ink Enduring

Book 6: Ink Exposed

Book 6.5: Adoring Ink

Book 6.6: Love, Honor, & Ink

Book 7: Inked Expressions

Book 7.3: Dropout

Book 7.5: Executive Ink

Book 8: Inked Memories

Book 8.5: Inked Nights

Book 8.7: Second Chance Ink

Book 8.5: Montgomery Midnight Kisses

Bonus: Inked Kingdom

The On My Own Series:

Book 0.5: My First Glance

Book 1: My One Night

Book 2: My Rebound

Book 3: My Next Play

Book 4: My Bad Decisions

The Promise Me Series:

Book 1: Forever Only Once

Book 2: From That Moment

Book 3: Far From Destined

Book 4: From Our First

The Less Than Series:

Book 1: Breathless With Her

Book 2: Reckless With You

Book 3: Shameless With Him

The Fractured Connections Series:

Book 1: Breaking Without You

Book 2: Shouldn't Have You

Book 3: Falling With You

Book 4: Taken With You

The Whiskey and Lies Series:

Book 1: Whiskey Secrets

Book 2: Whiskey Reveals

Book 3: Whiskey Undone

The Gallagher Brothers Series:

Book 1: Love Restored

Book 2: Passion Restored

Book 3: Hope Restored

The Ravenwood Coven Series:

Book 1: Dawn Unearthed

Book 2: Dusk Unveiled

Book 3: Evernight Unleashed

The Talon Pack:

Book 1: Tattered Loyalties

Book 2: An Alpha's Choice

Book 3: Mated in Mist

Book 4: Wolf Betrayed

Book 5: Fractured Silence

Book 6: Destiny Disgraced

Book 7: Eternal Mourning

Book 8: Strength Enduring

Book 9: Forever Broken

Book 10: Mated in Darkness

Book 11: Fated in Winter

Redwood Pack Series:

Book 1: An Alpha's Path

Book 2: A Taste for a Mate

Book 3: Trinity Bound

Book 3.5: A Night Away

Book 4: Enforcer's Redemption

Book 4.5: Blurred Expectations

Book 4.7: Forgiveness

Book 5: Shattered Emotions

Book 6: Hidden Destiny

Book 6.5: A Beta's Haven

Book 7: Fighting Fate

Book 7.5: Loving the Omega

Book 7.7: The Hunted Heart

Book 8: Wicked Wolf

The Elements of Five Series:

Book 1: From Breath and Ruin

Book 2: From Flame and Ash

Book 3: From Spirit and Binding

Book 4: From Shadow and Silence

Dante's Circle Series:

Book 1: Dust of My Wings

Book 2: Her Warriors' Three Wishes

Book 3: An Unlucky Moon

Book 3.5: His Choice

Book 4: Tangled Innocence

Book 5: Fierce Enchantment

Book 6: An Immortal's Song

Book 7: Prowled Darkness

Book 8: Dante's Circle Reborn

Holiday, Montana Series:

Book 1: Charmed Spirits

Book 2: Santa's Executive

Book 3: Finding Abigail

Book 4: Her Lucky Love

Book 5: Dreams of Ivory

The Branded Pack Series:

(Written with Alexandra Ivy)

Book 1: Stolen and Forgiven

Book 2: Abandoned and Unseen

Book 3: Buried and Shadowed

Dante's Circle Series:

Book 1: Dust of My Wings

Book 2: Her Warriors' Three Wishes

Book 3: An Unlikely Mate

Book 3.5: The Choice

Book 4: Tangled Innocence

Book 5: Fueled Enchantment

Book 6: An Immortal's Song

Book 7: Frosted Darkness

Book 8: Dante's Circle Reborn

Holiday, Montana Series:

Book 1: Charmed Spirits

Book 2: Santa's Executive

Book 3: Finding Abigail

Book 4: Her Lucky Love

Book 5: Dreaming of Jenna

The Branded Pack Series:

(Written with Alexandra Ivy)

Book 1: Stolen and Forgiven

Book 2: Abandoned and Unseen

ABOUT THE AUTHOR

Carrie Ann Ryan is the New York Times and USA Today bestselling author of contemporary, paranormal, and young adult romance. Her works include the Montgomery Ink, Redwood Pack, Fractured Connections, and Elements of Five series, which have sold over 3.0 million books worldwide. She started writing while in graduate school for her advanced degree in chemistry and hasn't stopped since. Carrie Ann has written over seventy-five novels and novellas with more in the works. When she's not losing herself in her emotional and action-packed worlds, she's reading as much as she can while wrangling her clowder of cats who have more followers than she does.

www.CarrieAnnRyan.com

Ingram Content Group UK Ltd.
Milton Keynes UK
UKHW041037230523
422204UK00004B/6/J